GALVESTON

A Novel

NIC PIZZOLATTO

Scribner

New York London Toronto Sydney

Scribner
A Division of Simon & Schuster, Inc.
1230 Avenue of the Americas
New York, NY 10020

First Scribner hardcover edition June 2010

For information about special discounts for bulk purchases,
please contact Simon & Schuster Special Sales at 1-866-506-1949
or business@simonandschuster.com.

The Simon & Schuster Speakers Bureau can bring authors to your live event. For more information or to book an event contact the Simon & Schuster Speakers Bureau at 1-866-248-3049 or visit our website at www.simonspeakers.com.

Designed by Carla Jayne Jones

Manufactured in the United States of America

1   3   5   7   9   10   8   6   4   2

Library of Congress Control Number: 2009042305

ISBN 978-1-4391-6664-2
ISBN 978-1-4391-6667-3 (ebook)

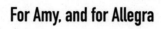

For Amy, and for Allegra

How often have I lain beneath rain on a strange roof, thinking of home.

—William Faulkner

ONE

A doctor took pictures of my lungs. They were full of snow flurries.

When I walked out the office all the people in the waiting room looked grateful they weren't me. Certain things you can see in a person's face.

I'd felt something was wrong because days before I had chased a guy up two flights of stairs and I'd had trouble breathing, like there was a barbell on my chest. I'd been drinking pretty hard for a couple weeks, but I knew it was more than that. I'd gotten so angry about the sudden pain that I broke the man's hand. He spat teeth and complained to Stan that he thought it was excessive.

But that's why they've always given me work. Because I'm excessive.

I told Stan about the chest pains and he sent me to a doctor who was into him for forty large.

Outside the doctor's office now I took the cigarettes from my jacket and started to crush the pack in my hands, but I decided this was no time to quit. I lit one up there on the sidewalk but it didn't taste good and the smoke made me think of cotton fibers weaving through my chest. Buses and cars cruised slow and daylight flashed off their glass and chrome. Behind my sunglasses it was kind of like I was at the bottom of the sea and the vehicles were fish. I imagined a much darker, cooler place, and the fish became shadows.

A horn jolted me awake. I'd started to step off the curb. I flagged down a taxi.

I was thinking about Loraine, a girl I'd once dated, and how one night I'd stayed up talking with her till dawn on a beach in Galveston, from a spot where we could watch the plump white exhaust from oil refineries unroll in the distance like a road into the sun. That would have been ten, eleven years ago. She was always too young for me, I guess.

Even before the X-rays I was already foul with anger because the woman I had thought of as my girlfriend, Carmen, had started sleeping with my boss, Stan Ptitko. I was on my way to meet him at his bar. Not much point today. But you don't stop being who you are just because there's a blizzard of soap chips in your chest.

There's no getting out alive, but you hope to avoid a deadline. I wasn't going to tell Stan or Angelo or Lou about my lungs. I didn't want them hanging out at the bar, talking about me when I wasn't there. Laughing.

Fingerprints smudged the cab's window, and uptown approached outside of it. Some places open themselves for you, but there was nothing gatelike about New Orleans. The city was a sunken anvil that sustained its own atmosphere. The sun flared between buildings and oak trees and I felt the light on my face and then the shade, like a strobe. I thought about Carmen's ass, and the way she smiled at me over her shoulder. I still thought about Carmen, and it didn't make sense because I knew she was a whore and totally heartless. She'd been with Angelo Medeiras when we started up. I guess I took her from him, more or less. Now she was with Stan. Angelo worked for him, too. It cooled my sense of insult to assume she was balling a few guys behind Stan's back.

I was trying to think of who I could tell about my lungs, because I wanted to tell someone. You have to admit that's a bullshit piece of news to get when you've got business to attend.

The bar was called Stan's Place, brick and tin-roofed, with barred windows and a dented metal door.

Lou Theriot, Jay Meires, and a couple people I didn't know sat inside, old guys. The bartender's name was George. His left ear was packed with white gauze. I asked him where Stan was and he nodded toward a set of stairs running up the wall to the office. The door was closed, so I sat on a stool and ordered a beer. Then I remembered that I was dying and changed the order to a Johnnie Walker Blue. Lou and Jay were talking about a problem with one of the bookmaking franchises. I could tell because I'd run book for a few years in my early twenties and knew the language. They stopped talking and looked up at me because I was listening. I didn't smile or anything and they went back to talking, but much softer now, with their heads turned down so I couldn't hear. They never cared much for me. They knew Carmen as a waitress here, before she hooked up with Stan, and I think they had some ill will toward me on her behalf.

They also didn't like me because I never really fit in around this crew. Stan inherited me from his former boss, Sam Gino, who inherited me from Harper Robicheaux, and it's mainly my fault that I wasn't ever fully accepted by these guys. They kept dago ideas about fashion—tracksuits or shirts with French cuffs, slicked hair—but I wear jeans and black T-shirts with a jacket and cowboy boots, like I always have, and I keep the back of my hair long and I won't shave my beard. My name's Roy Cady, but Gino started everyone calling me Big Country, and they still do, without affection. I'm from East Texas, the Golden Triangle, and these boys have always thought of me as trash, which is fine because they're also scared of me.

It's not like I had any desire to climb the corporational ladder.

I'd always gotten along fine with Angelo, though. Before the stuff with Carmen.

The office door opened then and Carmen stepped out, flattening her skirt and teasing her hair a bit, and right away she saw me and kind of froze. But Stan came out behind her and she walked down the stairs with him following, tucking his shirt at the back. Their footsteps made the stairs groan and Carmen lit a cigarette before she reached the bottom. She took it to the other end of the bar and ordered a greyhound.

I thought of a smart-ass remark to make to her, but I had to keep it to myself.

The main thing I was angry about was that she'd ruined my solitude. I'd been on my own for a long time.

I mean, I got laid when I needed it, but I was alone.

Now it was like alone didn't quite cut it.

Stan nodded to Lou and Jay, and he came to me and said that Angelo and I were going to do a job that night. It took effort for me to appear copacetic with this partnering. Stan had this sloped Polack brow like a cliff and it hung shadows over his tiny eyes.

He gave me a slip of paper and said, "Jefferson Heights. You're visiting Frank Sienkiewicz."

I remembered that name, a president or former president or attorney for the dockworkers' local.

The stevedores were supposedly coming under federal scrutiny, I think, rumored to be a probe target. They moved things for Stan's partners, and the payoffs kept their union alive, but that's really all I knew about it.

Stan said, "Nobody should get hurt bad. I don't want that now." He stood behind my stool, laid a hand on my shoulder. I could never read those small eyes stamped under the outcrop of his brow, but a secret to his success had to be the total lack of mercy in his face—the wide Slavic cheekbones over the tight, lipless mouth of a Cossack raider. If the Soviets really had people who'd run a red-hot coat hanger up inside the shaft of your cock, they were people like Stanislaw Ptitko. He said, "I need the guy to understand the right thing. He needs to play for the team. That's all."

"I need Angelo for that?"

"Take him anyway. Because I'm careful." He also told me that I needed to make a collection in Gretna before meeting Angelo. "So keep on schedule," he added, nodding to the Johnnie Walker in my hand.

Stan downed a shot of Stoli, slid the glass back to the bartender. The gauze around George's ear had a yellow stain at its center. Stan didn't really look at me as he straightened his tie and said, "No gats."

"What?"

"Remember that trucker last year? I don't want anybody getting shot because of someone's bullshit nerves. So I'm telling you and I'm telling Angelo: leave the guns. Don't let me find out you went in packing."

"The guy gonna be there?"

"He will. I'm sending him a care package."

He walked off and paused beside Carmen, kissed her hard and kneaded her tit once, and a barbaric intention crawled up in my mind. Then he walked out the back door and Carmen just looked bored, smoking. I thought about what Stan had said about not bringing guns.

Which struck me as a strange thing to say.

Carmen scowled at me from the other end of the bar, and Lou and Jay saw it and started talking to her, telling her how *relaxed* Stan seemed when he was with her. That was actually true, I realized, and it all started to tweak a bit and make places deep in the heart of me twinge with shame. I downed the JW and ordered another.

Carmen had light brown hair, long and bundled behind her head, and her pretty face had rough skin now and powder could build up in those little cracks and lines you couldn't see unless you were close to her. She reminded me of the empty glass of a swallowed cocktail, and at the heart of the empty glass was a smashed lime rind on ice.

I think the reason men liked her was because she gave off high levels of carnality. You looked at her and just knew—this one's up for anything. It's sexy, but you can't really stand it.

I knew about things she'd done, things Angelo didn't know about. Multiple-partner stuff. And one time she offered to bring an extra girl in for me, spice things up.

Not exactly my thing. At the time I had a sense of romance I now see was inappropriate.

I think she thrived on betrayal more than sex. Like she had a score to settle.

She claimed I hit her on one occasion, but I didn't believe it. She was a bit of an actress, and drama held more priority for her than the truth.

Though I admit my memory of the night in question is not quite whole.

In the bar then Lou said something to her like, "It's clear you know how to keep a man happy."

Carmen said, "Nobody can say I don't try."

They all laughed and the .380 at the small of my back felt like it was growing hot. It wouldn't have brought me any satisfaction. I was just angry, and I didn't want to die the way the doctor implied I would.

I dropped some bills on the bar and walked out. A couple nights back I'd been fried on tequila and left my truck here, and it was still intact, a big '84 F-150. This was in 1987, and I liked the models better then: squared and stocky, heavy machinery, not toys. I drove across the Pontchartrain Expressway and left the radio off and my thoughts hummed like a bee's wings.

Gretna. On Franklin Street I wondered when the last time I did things would be. Every beat of sunlight that struck the windshield as the trees passed kind of demanded that I appreciate it, but I can't say that I did. I tried to conceive of not existing, but I didn't have the imagination for it.

I felt that same choking and hopeless sense as when I was twelve, thirteen, staring down the long fields of cotton. August mornings with the burlap sack slung over my shoulder, and Mr. Beidle on his horse with the coach's whistle, directing the kids from the group home. The miserable idea of endlessness in the task. That feeling like You Cannot Win. After a week of picking I first noticed the calluses on my hands when I dropped a fork and realized I couldn't feel anything with my fingertips. I looked at the hard pads on my fingers now, wrapping the steering wheel, and a wave of anger clenched them. A feeling like I'd been cheated. Then I thought of Mary-Anne, my mother. She was weak, a clever woman who willed herself stupid. But there was no need to think on her today.

I found the address Stan had given me, a sinkhole apartment building next to a line of warehouses: pale, graffitied brick, high weeds and crabgrass blending into the vacant lot next door. Clunkers in the parking lot, that air of oil and hot garbage that circles New Orleans.

Number 12. Second floor. Ned Skinner.

I strolled past his window once and glanced inside. It was dark and I didn't register any movement. I slipped a hand in the pocket where I stored my knuckle-dusters and kept on walking across the balcony. I went downstairs, around back, and checked his outside windows. A breeze wavered the high weeds.

I walked back up and knocked on his door. The whole building had a deserted vibe; blinds stayed closed, no noise from TVs or radios. So I waited and looked around and then used my switchblade on the frame around the lock. Cheap wood, splintered easy.

I slipped in and shut the door. A small place with a couple pieces of furniture and trash everywhere, newspapers and a ton of old racing forms, fast-food wrappers, a dial television with a cracked screen. Empty bottles of well-brand vodka stood along the counter. I always did hate a slob.

It smelled bad in there, like sweat and stale breath and human vinegar. Mildew and dirt singed the bathroom, stiff clothes on the tiles. The bedroom had just a mattress on the floor and thin, yellowed sheets in a tangle. Crumbled racing forms scattered over the carpet like cut flowers.

On the floor by the bed a framed picture lay on its back. I picked it up: a brown-haired woman with a little boy, both cute enough, smiling and bright-eyed. It looked several years old. You could tell by the woman's hairstyle and fashion, and the paper was of thicker stock than you usually saw nowadays, a leathery texture, and it seemed the faces had faded some over time. I carried it into the living room and threw a pizza box off a chair and sat. I looked down at the picture and then at the apartment. I'd lived in places like this.

I studied the smiles in the picture.

Something passed close to me then, a feeling or piece of knowledge, but I couldn't quite get it. A sense of something I'd once known or felt, a memory that wouldn't come into the light. I kept reaching, but I couldn't grasp the thing.

It felt near, though.

The light from the blinds poured across me in old-fashioned prison stripes. I waited for a long time in that chair, but the man never showed. And given what happened later, I'd come to view the time spent waiting for him as a demarcation in each of our lives, his and mine.

A moment when things could have gone one way, before they went another.

met up with Angelo at eight that night, in the Blue Horse off Tchoupitoulas Street. It was a kind of biker bar and I always felt at home there, more than in Stan's Place.

I'd stopped by my trailer first. I had this idea, and it was sort of paranoid, but when Stan told me not to bring guns, I'd started thinking. I wondered why he told me that when I'm a pro and not even a button man, really. And why he needed me to do this with Angelo. I had this idea I was being set up for Angelo. Maybe he and Stan both wanted to do me over something with Carmen. Like they believed I'd hit her. Or just didn't want me walking around having screwed her. Or something.

Just to say it didn't feel right. It didn't matter if I questioned my instincts, I was still going to follow them. So I packed my brass knuckles and collapsible baton, but I also tucked the Colt Mustang .380 I favored into my boot. Plus I strapped a spring-loaded stiletto onto my forearm. I hadn't used the thing in years, but I oiled it with WD-40 and tried it out with my jacket on, and when I twisted my wrist that blade shot into my hand like a shard of cold lightning.

Angelo surprised me when I met him at the bar, though. He

turned on his stool and stuck out his hand. He wore a blasted, hangdog look on his face, and so I shook his hand, being very careful not to twist my wrist.

"You ready to do this?" I said.

"Let me finish." He turned back to the bar and sipped his highball. His thinning pompadour sat far back on his forehead, and with the black jogging suit he stuck out here the way I stuck out at Stan's. I sat beside him and stared at the bottles.

He looked over at me with what I'd describe as a furious sadness, like he could hardly sit still and didn't know what to do with himself, bouncing his knee, picking at his manicure. Then I got it.

"Problems?" I said.

"You know about Stan and Carmen?" he asked.

"Of course. Yeah."

He glowered at me.

"Fuck it," I said. I looked at the bottles and remembered my cancer. "Double Johnnie Walker Blue."

The drink cost forty dollars. It was hot and smooth down my throat, and it spread warmth through my chest and made my chest feel alive.

"She's just . . ." Angelo muttered.

"What?" I said.

"*How* she—she's just going to—*why*? With *him*? You know the same stories as me about him."

I said, "She's not the purest chick, exactly. I mean, come on. She's a slut."

"Don't say that. I don't need to talk about her like that."

"Then don't talk about her at all," I said. "Not with me." From the corner of my eye, I could see him glaring at me.

13

The other thing men liked about Carmen was that she was smart, or at any rate cunning, and clever about the ways men thought. It was hard to write her off as a bimbo. I think a lot of guys thought she was smarter than them, and that can be kind of exciting. I guzzled the last half of the fantastic whisky and spun around.

"You ready?"

I almost thought he'd take a shot at me, but he sighed and nodded in defeat, hoisted himself up and had to steady his legs. I hadn't realized he was that drunk, and now I was a little worried about the man in Jefferson Heights, Sienkiewicz. "You drive," he said.

My truck shimmied awake like a wet dog, and the radio's voice was in the middle of saying something about Jim Bakker getting defrocked. Angelo sat as if deflated. I double-checked the address and took Napoleon north to 90.

He leaned forward and shut off my radio. "You remember," he said, his voice a little sloshed. "You remember, like years ago, when we broke up those kids selling in Audubon Park?"

I thought a minute. "Yeah."

"Man. That boy that just started crying. You remember—I mean, we hadn't even done anything. And the *tears* just—" He giggled.

"I remember."

"*Please. It's just to pay for school.*"

"Yep."

"And you say, 'This *is* school.'" He paused, straightened himself in the seat. "You remember that bag?"

"Oh yeah."

This was about five years back, just after I'd moved over to

14

Stan's crew. The kid had had a knapsack stuffed with four thousand dollars and little quarter baggies of blow.

"You remember what we did?" Angelo asked.

"Gave it to Stan."

"Yeah." He shifted to face me, hands limp in his lap. "I know you thought the same thing as me. That we could just split it. That Stan didn't need to know."

His weak, meandering voice merged with the car lights that flashed across the windshield.

"But we didn't trust each other," he went on. "We both thought about it. But we didn't *trust*."

I glanced at him and took a deep breath. "What are you getting at?"

He shrugged. "I don't know. I'm just—I been *thinking*. I mean. What do I have to show? What do *you* have to show? I'm forty-three, man."

It was like he just expected a pal, and I didn't think he had the right. Plus it was pretty pitiful to hear this fat wop trying to talk about his feelings when he didn't even have the vocabulary to label them.

Him whining about his life when I'd been fitted for a coffin.

I said, "Why don't you just get yourself focused?"

"Huh."

He stared out the window and I put in a tape of Billy Joe Shaver, which I knew Angelo hated, but he didn't say anything about the music.

I felt a little guilty because I'd kind of planned to stab him in the neck tonight, but that would have been about the same as kicking a cripple. You'd need a good reason.

I have a sense of fair play.

Meaning, if I'm given your name on a piece of paper, it's because you did something to put it in my hand. Something you shouldn't have done.

Anyway, Angelo just stared out the window and sighed like a teenage girl while I felt the steel guitar pulse up from the door speakers and tingle my fillings. After a while I found the house, a Victorian on Newman Avenue with a yard fenced by wrought iron spears. We circled the block a few times, expanding outward to check if the place was under surveillance. I put the truck on Central so we could creep over between houses.

I checked my gear and stuffed my ski mask in my jacket pocket. Angelo started to put his on and I told him to wait till we got there, which he knew to do, but he was acting like he couldn't tie his shoes, and I was thinking about just telling him to wait for me. That wouldn't do, though, and we both slipped through the yards to the other side. Only one streetlight burned on Newman, and it was down past the place we were going. I didn't hear any dogs and the lights were off in the house.

I told him I'd go around the back and he should knock on the front.

I slipped on my mask, placed my hands between the posts, and vaulted over the fence, through a quiet backyard with a little stone pond that trickled, and its sound was calming and strange. I climbed the stairs to the back door, and I didn't think about it at the time, but I should have noticed there were no motion lights or anything. I hadn't noticed that of all the houses on the street, this particular one was draped in darkness.

But I was in a hurry. I could taste my whisky breath trapped by the mask and I could hear it rasping under the burble of that stone pond, and I stood against the back door and listened.

I heard Angelo's knock on the other side of the house and waited, felt footsteps inside walking to the front door. I stepped back, flipped out my baton, and counted three seconds. Then my boot cracked the door and the wood crashed inward.

I charged into darkness blind, the baton raised. Something heavy thudded my skull and red bloomed out of the dark.

I lost time.

I woke up when someone dropped me on the floor, a migraine kicking my head. My mask was off and I saw Angelo sitting across from me. His face was runny with blood, and he lifted a hand to his nose. We were in the foyer outside the front door, tinted mustard by a tiny lamp on the wall that gave off a scrap of light beneath orange glass. Red wallpaper. A man stood beside me, and another beside Angelo. They wore black jumpsuits and ski masks and each held a handgun fitted with a silencer. They had black vests with bulging pockets and rugged combat boots. Real professional. Their eyes locked with mine, small and cold, like Stan's.

The one beside Angelo glanced around the wall and we heard footsteps. I thought a woman whimpered. A tang of gunpowder wound through the air, and also the smell of shit. I looked around.

What had to be Sienkiewicz's body lay off to the side in the next room. His shirt gleamed wetly.

I heard another sob and thought it was Angelo, but my eyes adjusted and I saw a girl sitting on a chair in the dark, in the room to my left. I could see enough of her cheeks to make out the mascara that ran over them. She was clutching herself and shaking.

I understood what was going on and why Stan hadn't wanted

us to bring guns. I looked to Angelo, but he seemed baffled, his eyes wet and useless, staring at the blood his palm collected beneath his nose.

Footsteps came closer and a third man walked around the corner, buckling his pants. He carried a thick folder full of papers pressed under his arm, and he dressed like the other two, hardcore. After he'd hitched his pants he pulled his gun from his waistband.

"Stand them up." He had a weird accent, not American or European.

Angelo hollered, "What is this? Who are you?" One of the men swatted his face with the butt of his gun, and Angelo covered his mouth and rolled back and forth on the ground.

The girl in the chair started breathing faster and harder, like she was choking.

The man who'd hit him grabbed Angelo's hair and pulled him to his feet. The one beside me put his silencer on my temple and said, "Up."

I rose slow and his gun stayed on me. I could feel they'd emptied my pockets and the .380 wasn't in my boot anymore. I glanced at Angelo. He stood in a little puddle of piss. It was close quarters with three guns and we were unarmed.

People simply do not make it out of things like that.

They moved Angelo over against one wall, measuring the space between him and Sienkiewicz's body in the next room. I think they were trying to pose us so it might look like we all killed one another, but I don't know.

The man beside me slapped the side of my head, then he shoved me forward and I acted like I stumbled, fell to one knee. When he tugged me to my feet I flicked my wrist and whipped the stiletto into his neck. Blood geysered hot over my face and mouth.

I left the blade in and fell behind him as the other two raised guns. One shot at me and smacked plaster off a wall as the other fired at Angelo and the top of his pompadour flew off and he fell to his knees. They both fired at me. The shots went *thwap* like pneumatic bolts and all struck the third man. He spasmed at the bullets, the blade still in his neck.

My gun was right in front of me, stuck in the man's waistband. I pulled it out and raised it and fired through the blood fountain at the closest one.

I didn't have time to actually aim, and I was half-blind with arterial spray, but I hit him in the throat and he twitched and fired and dropped backward.

I never shot like that in my life.

And this—the last man, the one who'd clipped Angelo, his buddy had shot *him* on the way down. His armpit smoldered and he gripped himself, slumped against the wall. His gun sat a few feet away from his boot.

Angelo's body finished falling then, thumped sideways on the carpet.

The last man looked at his gun, his foot, and then at me, just as I shot him in the head.

The whole thing took maybe five seconds.

Smoke spread over the foyer like ground fog. The top of Angelo's face had broken off, his cheeks slicked with tears and blood. I threw up. The girl in the chair cried louder, made a moaning sound.

The three men in black were piled on the floor and thin tendrils of smoke rose from their bodies. The blade stuck from the one's neck like a big thorn, and the orange light made his flowing blood look like paint.

The girl in the shadows just sat shivering wide-eyed in her chair. I passed her and walked around the hall.

I saw a light in a room toward the back and crept toward it. A woman's naked body sprawled on a bed, tinted green by a reading lamp on the nightstand. The sheets were bloodied and she had deep bruises around her throat and thighs. She was young, but not as young as the girl in the chair.

I walked back to that girl and said, "Get up. I'm not going to hurt you."

She didn't move. She wasn't looking at me or even blinking. I had to let her sit there a second while I wiped blood from my eyes.

I noticed the folder of papers splayed across the foyer floor, bone fragments spattered on them. I crouched and gathered them up and started for the back door, but I stopped. The girl hadn't moved.

She'd seen my face, though. I slapped her cheek. I pulled her off the chair by her arm. "Get up. You're coming with me."

She stuttered, "What are you going to do?"

"We have to get out of here."

"Where are we going?"

"I don't know." I stared at her face clearly for the first time. She was younger than I'd have guessed. She wore her mascara clumsily, too much of it, like spilled ink now. Blond, very short hair, and even with the makeup running down her cheeks she looked almost childish, and there was something else there, too, something like what you could see in Carmen's eyes at times—rules for self-preservation, a knot of hard choices. I could have imagined it. Whatever I recognized only fluttered past me as instinct or sentiment.

"Come with me," I said. When she didn't move I held the gun in her face.

She stared down the barrel and then at my eyes. I couldn't tell what color her eyes were in the low orange light. She looked at the floor. Then she kneeled down off the chair and crouched around the bodies, going through the pockets of the men I'd killed. I reckoned she was searching for money, or something they'd taken from her. I could appreciate that, as it seemed to confirm what I'd sensed about her pragmatic streak.

The whole time I waited for sirens. I stepped to the windows and looked out, but the night appeared still and untroubled. The girl had gathered a big purse from the side room and stuffed some things in it when she was done rifling pockets. She rose up with a fierce, sober look. "Vonda," she said. "My friend Vonda."

She started to walk down the hall, toward the bedroom, and I grabbed her wrist. I shook my head. "You don't want to see that."

"But—"

I tugged her by the arm out the back door, then across the street and into the shadows, where I still kept waiting to hear sirens from Highway 90. Blood and gunpowder stuffed my nostrils and I could feel the blood drying on my cheeks. I pulled off my shirt and rubbed hard at my face, blew my nose. We slipped between the yards and through the trees' spotty darkness and we were out of sight.

When we reached the truck I pushed her inside and started the engine. Billy Joe's singing mixed with the engine noise, and the sounds made me grin. It occurred to me that if I had told

Stan about my lungs all of this might not have happened. He might have decided to let nature take its course.

For a second I just sat in the truck, grinning from ear to ear. I guess this scared the girl, because she cringed against the window, faced the floor as I pulled away from the curb and steered us toward the highway.

Now in hindsight I think there must have been more to my bringing her than just that she'd seen my face. Because what did I care if she saw my face? I was dying. I could have shaved my beard, cut my hair. I mean, one of the reasons for keeping my hair long was because if I got jammed up, I could give myself a crew cut and shave and the whole profile would change.

I think that maybe for a second there, in that foyer with its burnt orange light filled with smoke and blood and the gunshot still ringing in my ears, my jaw rigid with adrenaline, something about her face, the fear and grief in her face, was like the feeling that struck me in that empty apartment earlier—the sensation of a thing forgotten but resonating, an intuitional memory, an absence.

Anyway, it turned out this girl was from East Texas, too.

The girl said her name was Raquel and everyone called her Rocky. She was mostly terrified, and given what she'd been through, a lot of people might have switched off, but she talked like a mynah bird. I suspect that sometime before the night's events, she had learned that you can live with anything. "My last name's Arceneaux." She pronounced it *Arson, oh*. "Are you going to kill me?"

"No. Stop asking me that."

I drove us to my trailer in Metairie. We sat at the edge of the trailer park for a while, in the dark, but my double-wide looked the way I'd left it. No vehicles I didn't recognize. No light in the windows. So we walked in. I pressed her ahead and kept the lights off.

"*This* is where you live?"

"Shut up."

I wondered how long ago the men in commando gear were supposed to check in with Stan. Outside the world was almost too still; the live oak and maple surrounding the park didn't seem to rustle, just hung over these little boxes in an unmoving air, and the lights in the other trailers didn't reveal any motion. No one passed in the windows, their lusterless glow lighting the undersides of branches and the plastic toys and tires pocking the muddy yards. I turned on the hall light.

I left my gun on the lid of the septic tank and washed my face in the bathroom sink, scrubbed my forearms and hands with Lava soap and blistering water that drained in a pink whirl.

I grabbed a fresh shirt and from my closet dug out a small lockbox like the kind used in banks for safe deposits. It contained a little over three thousand dollars and a fake driver's license and passport I'd had made years ago. My retirement plan. I also took a box of .380 shells from one shelf, a clean license plate, some more clothes, and threw it all in an old army-surplus duffel bag.

The girl sat in the living room's single chair, a large La-Z-Boy where I'd end up sleeping most nights. An army of empty High Life cans covered the floor around the chair—an actual army, because I'd used a knife to cut little strips out of the can sides so that they folded down, like arms, and I'd pulled the tops upright to resemble heads. I'd done all that while watching *Fort Apache,* and it was a little embarrassing to have her see. The chair faced my television and VCR and the tape collection beside it.

"You got a lot of movies," she said. "But no furniture." Her eyes scanned the beer cans on the rug.

I wagged the gun at her. "Get back to the truck. Move."

"We just got here. All your movies are *old.*"

I had a nearly complete collection of John Wayne on tape, and I was sorry to leave it. It had taken me a few years to put together.

"It's not safe," I said. "Move. Or we'll have a problem."

At the truck I used a screwdriver to switch my license plate with the good one I'd had stamped years ago; it corresponded to a dentist's Ford in Shreveport.

The thing to do would be to just get on I-10 and drive west till we were out of Louisiana. We could have gone east, but I'm not welcome in the state of Mississippi, and less than four hours west and you're in Texas, which I preferred.

I dumped my duffel in the truck bed. The lockbox and the folder from Sienkiewicz's house I kept behind the seat. We merged onto the interstate.

"So why'd those men want to kill you?" she said.

"Some bullshit. Over a woman." I smacked the steering wheel and realized how pissed I was about that. "That's what my life's worth."

She wanted to hear more about it, but I wouldn't spill. I asked her how she came to be doing what she did. By this point I understood that she was a whore, her and her friend sent to ground Sienkiewicz at home.

She said, "You still got some blood on your face."

I looked in the rearview and then her small finger touched under my jaw. "Right there," she said.

I wiped at it with a little spit. The other side of the tape played Loretta Lynn and the spot on my jaw where she'd touched me pulsed with a slight warmth. I tried to keep her talking because she'd be easier to deal with, and I didn't want her any deeper in shock. Maybe I just wanted to hear someone's voice. It was all starting to sink in, and it's possible I wanted someone to talk to me. I said, "Go on. What you were saying."

"What's that?"

"How you came to be where you were."

"Oh. Well." She'd already told me that she was from Orange, Texas, right on the Louisiana border and not far from Port Arthur, where I'd grown up. She claimed to be eighteen. She'd ran off about five months ago, she said, following a boy a few years older to New Orleans.

"He was kind of a disaster. Toby. Wasn't a worse dude I could of hitched on with. He said he knew all these people in the city could get us jobs. And made it sound like he was real connected, like. He was queer, so I thought he was telling the truth. All he ended up doing as far as work was running little packages of dope for some people around St. Roch and the Lower Ninth. Then he has this idea he's going to like *skim* off some of it. Cut it, you know. Build up his own stash. This was not a good time for me. One day I don't see him no more. He doesn't come back to the room. I don't know if he died or just had to run off because he'd done something. But he was gone."

She picked her lip and stared out at the passing night with a face that quivered on the verge of haywire, like a leaf shuddering in a high wind. "Nobody ever came looking for him. I was fed up by then. But I was also almost out of money. He didn't leave me any. I knew a girl." She paused again and shivered a little, a spasm jerking down her spine, and she covered her mouth.

"What?"

Her face twisted up, and she began crying. She wiped her eyes and straightened her shoulders. "I knew this girl named Vonda. She was in the same hotel. She told me she worked for herself. She was, well. You know what I'm saying. I didn't know anything about that stuff, but the way Vonda talked—it was funny. And it seemed kind of all right, because it was even listed in the phone book. Elite Escorts. Like a real business. And she told me, she said, 'If you do something good, never do it for free.' Isn't that funny? It almost makes sense, huh?"

She turned to me. "You know, you remind me of somebody. A dude in one of those bands my stepdad used to like. The Almond Brothers. Some guy on the cover of the record."

I said, "One of the owners of Elite Escorts is a guy named Stan Ptitko. You ever met him?"

"No. I think, maybe, I might of heard the name a couple times. I mean, I'm still new. Who is that?"

"He's the guy that tried to have me killed tonight."

"Oh."

"You were talking about your friend. Vonda."

"Yeah." Her eyes brimmed and the dash lights floated in them. "Vonda was good to me. I met some other girls she knew. This happened real recent, like. I couldn't make rent. I mean, I was kind of stuck. But—but she—" She shook her head as if denying a charge, covered her mouth.

"That was Vonda," I said. "In the house? In the bedroom."

She nodded her head, her small, muscled shoulders quaking. I let her do that a while.

When she was able to talk she said, "They told us it'd be easy. Just the two of us to work this one dude. Right as he started up with Vonda, them three fellas bust in. And when they came in, Vonda was undressing—I was taking longer—and they . . . They wouldn't let her put her clothes on. They hit that guy some, until he showed them where something was. Then they just shot him.

"But Vonda—she was naked, like. And we were both freaking out. I never seen anything like that. They. Um. *They*—" She shook her head again, balled a tiny fist and struck her thigh with

27

it over and over. She had nice legs and I didn't think she should bruise them. "They took her in the bedroom. They said—they made me sit down. They said they were, they were—" She stuttered badly as she went on. "They said I was the after-party. Oh *God*—I'm—*oh*—" She gritted her teeth and clutched her stomach like she'd been punched. "I am *so, so* glad you killed those fuckers, man."

"I'm glad too."

She rubbed her palms in her eyes. She was fine-boned, and even upset she had a rugged toughness that was pure country— a dumb, furious pride I recognized. Then I realized something.

I hadn't thought about my cancer in a while. More than that, I felt *good*. Like I was some kind of hero.

Like I had saved her.

And I was also thinking about the idea of luck, and how perfectly I'd shot. How lucky I'd been that they hadn't found the stiletto or that the trigger hadn't flipped when they knocked me out and dragged me to the foyer.

I let Rocky cry and dig her nails into her thighs with as much privacy as the truck allowed. I put in a Roy Orbison tape.

Depending on the places we passed, the night around us shaded from ink black to red and purple to a washed-out yellow that hung like gauze in front of the dark, like you could see the dark sitting under the light, and then it would be back to ink black, and the air would change smells from sea salt to pine pulp to ammonia and burning oil. Trees and marshland crowded us and we passed over the Atchafalaya Basin, a long bridge suspended over a liquid murk, and I thought about the dense congestion of vines and forest when I was a kid, how the green and leafy things had seemed so full of shadows, and how it had felt like half the world was hidden in those shadows.

Refinery towers burned in the night and their trail of bright gray smoke made me picture Loraine sitting on that beach in Galveston, with her head cradled on my chest, telling her about the cotton fields. I wondered what she would think about this.

I'd paid a man to find out where she was, a few years back. She'd gotten married. I still had her new name and address written down, and now and then I thought to go look her up. But it was ten years ago, and I was always too old for her.

Around Lafayette, Rocky had pulled herself together again and her disposition had veered to a kind of excitement that put me on guard. Those quick reversals of mood you saw in women had always struck me as staged, suspicious.

"Where we going now?" she asked.

"I'll drop you off after we cross Texas. I can drop you in Orange, if you want. You can go back to your family."

"Uh-uh. I ain't going back there. You better just drop me off right here."

"Somewhere else then, if not Orange. But you stay with me till Texas. Those men'll be looking for you. They're gonna want to find out what happened back there. You know what that means?"

The way she sank back into the seat I could tell she'd begun to understand how different things were now. "Oh."

The random lights passed over her face, and her eyes glimmered like the muddy marsh beneath us. She chewed her lip in a scheming way.

"Then let's go somewhere together," she said.

"How's that?"

She twisted sideways, a surge of animation when her legs crossed up on the seat, the skirt tugged high on lean thighs. "Look—you were just saying you're running, now, huh? And I'm running—you just said, huh? We're from the same parts, man. Why don't we just run together a little while and see how it goes?"

The back of my neck grew hot and something caught in my throat, but I didn't let on. I glanced over at her legs, her blond hair clipped above her neck and crimped into feathery locks, parted around her face, her face sharp and birdlike, with big eyes whose color I still couldn't locate. She'd reapplied her makeup and still used too much mascara, trying to make herself look older, I guess, but the fat clumps of eyelash made her look more like a kid.

Probably she was the sort of country tail that went nuts if there wasn't a man around.

"I'm just saying," she said, ducking her eyes. "I'd feel a lot *safer* right now if I could stick with you a little while."

I shook my head. "No way. Jesus. *No.* Where you think we'd go?"

"I don't know." She shrugged. "Somewhere on the Gulf? Somewhere with beaches? Corpus, maybe? Or what about all the way west? Huh? *California.*" She grinned, and it bothered me that she talked like this was a vacation.

"How much money do you have?" I asked.

She drew her face back. "Me? About zero to none."

"*Ah,*" I said.

She squared her shoulders. "You think I want *your* money, shitkicker? I can get my own bank just fine. I *had* my own money but it's back there. In New Orleans. You didn't *ask* if I needed to run by *my* place. You're the one kidnapped *me.*" She folded her arms, scowled, tokens of that stupid, spiteful pride, mustered by hard years. "I don't need your damn money."

"Then you don't need me, Rocky. You could disappear a whole lot easier if you weren't tied to me."

"Yeah. *Disappear.*" She shifted her legs and faced the windshield again. "I don't know. I don't really want to be alone, all right? Right now—I mean, given everything—I don't really want to be alone. Okay?"

Red lights erupted in my rearview, crashing out the night like a gunshot or a scream. Sirens. She gasped.

"It's all right," I said, but my heart was about to buck out my sternum and I turned the radio off, braked, and drifted to the side of the road. She pulled her purse to her lap and clutched it with both hands.

"Don't let them arrest us," she said, and her voice was not soft or scared, but hard and without compromise. "Don't you let them do it, man."

But as I pulled to the shoulder the cop flew past us, shrieking and flashing, and it was one of the prettiest sights I ever saw, that smokey's lights blinking smaller and smaller in the distance.

Our breathing was the only sound then. Her hands unclenched her purse and we started laughing. She had a shrill, hysterical laugh that made her mouth drop open like a trapdoor. I waited till the cop's lights vanished and then I moved the truck onto the road.

We drove in silence awhile. "There's no good reason for us to stick together," I said. I didn't really know why I brought the subject up again.

What I came to see later was that I was asking her to convince me, to give me an excuse. Like an unmade part of me saw its chance to be born.

She said, "How about, I don't know, *solidarity*, man? We're like partners in crime now."

"Really, really different crimes."

"Whatever." She faced the window and folded her arms. She was done trying to talk me into it, but maybe that was only because she could tell I was easy.

I said, "Tell me why you don't want to go to Orange."

Her chin set out and she said, "Don't worry about it. I got my reasons."

"Your family still there?"

She rolled her eyes and sighed, "Some."

"You can't go to them?"

"We're not close, man. All right?" She squeezed the purse to her belly and sucked her bottom lip.

"Mother and father?"

"Stepdad. What, dude, are you just going to go digging at this stuff? Come on. What do you care?"

"Take it easy. It's just your stepfather?"

The forest swayed around the interstate and she crooked her jaw. "Look, if I talk at you because you tell me I have to, there's no way you can know if I'm lyin' or not, man. *Anyway*. So just let it all go, all right? I mean, how'd *you* get to New Orleans?"

I raised the radio volume and she settled back, but in my head an answer arranged itself. My own history had always seemed arbitrary to me.

I'd worked for Harper Robicheaux in Beaumont since I was seventeen. After he died in '77, in Breaux Bridge, Louisiana,

Sam Gino bought into the action. Then Stan Ptitko was pulled in to run the bar. Then later there was no more Sam Gino but his people still wanted to give me work. In the city. That was the answer to how I got to New Orleans.

I thought about that. It was true, but the story didn't feel correct. It didn't really explain anything, did it?

I was seven when John Cady got back from Korea, and less than two years later he'd fallen off a cooling tower at the refinery and broken his neck, drunk before noon. I called him dad but as I grew older several things made it pretty obvious he was not my father—our looks, the timeline of my conception. He was always kind to me, though we didn't know each other long. Around a year after we buried him Mary-Anne dropped off a bridge. She preferred me to call her Mary-Anne instead of Mom, which she claimed aged a woman ten years. They said she jumped, but I don't believe the people she was with are to be trusted. Then the group home and the Beidles and the cotton fields.

And now I was dying and everything that had ever happened to me was starting to seem hazily important.

Lake Charles transpired after three hours on the road, and the lights beyond the trees grew brighter.

She sat up. "Where are we stopping tonight? How far are we going?"

"I haven't decided. My main thing was to get out of there. It's looking like we got away."

"I think maybe so."

"I was thinking, it might take a while for them to find out what happened, to figure it out. But when they do—what? It's not like the cops have our info. They couldn't give us to the law without screwing themselves. This guy, Stan Ptitko. People know who he is. He doesn't want this noise."

"Okay."

"So if we keep low and keep getting farther away . . . Yeah. We'll probably get away."

She nodded. "I mean, though, are we driving to New Mexico or Nevada or what?"

"I don't know." Neither of us acted like we noticed that I didn't argue about her sticking around.

"You know, if you cut your hair and shaved your beard I bet no one would recognize you."

"I'm aware."

"I kind of want a drink."

"I kind of want several. Like a pitcher of single malt."

She faced me and laid her knees on the seat. "It's starting to feel like I never needed a drink as bad in my life as I do now."

"Well, you're young yet."

Her eyebrows played in a mischievous, slutty way, too much so. It was a thin mask, because she also looked tired and stunned and close to ruin, and like she was fighting it all by jigging those eyebrows.

The tape had run out and the tires hummed on the pavement. We were almost out of the city and nearing Sulphur, where the long shoreline of refineries looked like Chicago at night. I thought about a couple places I knew in Lake Charles. "You got ID?" I said.

She nodded.

It was slightly unreal, a little dreamlike, as the pavement descended and the trees peeled away onto the bright yellow streetlights of the main drag, Prien Lake Road.

I found a place I'd been to years before called John's Barn. Kind of small, it had a low ceiling and three pool tables, stuffed with fat women and angry men drinking Miller Lite and waiting for a fight. Lake Charles was one of the easiest places to get your ass kicked on the Gulf Coast. And any place south of here was a white-trash terror camp.

We drove around the gravel parking lot and I put the truck in the shadows under some trees in back. Smoke flowed over the women's tall, stiff curls like fog around icebergs. The national and confederate flags hung along a back wall above a picture of Ronnie Reagan and his heroic hair. I caught Waylon playing on the juke and laughter and friendly voices chattered around, so it looked okay.

A few people gave us looks, as she was young enough to be my daughter. But maybe she was, for all they knew. The bartender wore the collar of his shirt turned up, and he'd torn off the sleeves. He looked between her ID and her face about ten times.

I ordered a bottle of Bud and a shot of JW.

Rocky stood on her tiptoes and tapped her fingers at the bar. "You got grapefruit juice?" The guy nodded. His mustache was thin and sickly looking, his hair flat and parted like an accountant's. "What kind?" she asked. "Yellow or pink?"

He reached into a cooler and lifted a tiny can. "Yellow."

"Cool," she said. "Let me get a double salty dog, extra salt." It was the kind of order that can earn you ill will in a place like that, but I saw she had a high-beam smile she could throw out, the kind that could break a scowl. I didn't much care for the way he smiled back at her, though.

Everyone at the counter had stopped talking to look at us.

They were all drinking Bud or Miller and probably took offense at the hint of pretension in our order. Only a few tables stood in the center of the place and they were all taken, so we went and leaned against a rail along the wall in back.

We finished our drinks in maybe five minutes.

She said, "Four or five more of those and I might be okay."

"Tell me about it."

She slid me her empty glass. "Could you spot me? Just for tonight."

I nodded. But as I walked to the bar to pay for the next round old instincts were already raising my hackles. The first and most useful rule of prison is that you do your own time, not somebody else's.

Everybody watched me order, and the bartender didn't make the salty dog with the same cheerful demeanor. When I returned two boys stood by Rocky, leaning on pool sticks and grinning dumbly while she gave them that easy smile and twisted an ankle.

I set the drinks on the rail.

"Hey," she said. "Thanks. This is Curtis and David."

They were both skinny and rawboned, both wore ball caps low over the flat, narrow faces and small, close-set eyes I've always associated with bayou-country inbreeding. I nodded, acknowledged the bitter awareness that flickered across their faces.

"They work at the plants in Sulphur," she said. "Curtis rides in rodeo."

"Yeah," said one, holding out his hand for a shake. "What're y'all doing around here?"

I shook his hand. "Nice to meet you." Then I turned my back on them. I could see by Rocky's face that they were still behind me and I looked over my shoulder.

"Hey," the one said, "y'all want to play some pool?"

"No thanks." I turned around. "You boys beat it."

Their chests puffed and eyes slanted to stab wounds. They looked between them and back to me with tiny cold stares, dumb and black as a fish's. I'd known dudes like this my whole life, country morons stuck in a state of permanent resentment. They abuse small animals, grow up to beat their kids with belts and wreck their trucks driving drunk, find Jesus at forty and start going to church and using prostitutes.

"No reason to be rude, mister."

Rocky said, "Oh, *please*, y'all. Don't worry about it. My uncle's okay."

They glanced at each other while I stared at them, and I felt that tiny vein in my forehead jumping double-time. Then they stopped trying to look me in the eye. The boys gave her a sort of courtesy nod, loped back to their game without turning around.

"Jeez, man," she said. "What's up with you?"

I sipped my JW. "We aren't trying to meet people here. You understand me?"

"Well, you tearing them guys' heads off wouldn't exactly have been low-profile."

I didn't reply, but I marked how easily and quickly I'd located the rage that would have enabled me to maybe cripple those boys.

That was kind of my thing. Always had been.

It stayed close to the surface with me.

But it wasn't righteous now, given the situation and this girl being who she was. The boys regarded us from the pool table, talking to themselves. I sipped my beer and stared at a poster of the Saints cheerleaders on the wall. The way Rocky looked at me had changed, gotten more wary, and the light from the jukebox streamed over her face and caught in her eyes. I looked at them.

"What?" she said.

"You got green eyes. I wondered."

"Hell, man. You're kind of odd."

I lit a cigarette. "Why'd you wave them over?"

"Well, I was going to bum a cigarette from them. But I'll just take one of yours." She reached into my jacket pocket and pulled out a pack of Camels, took one and replaced the pack, and the whole series of gestures seemed very calculated and amateurish.

"You're not telling the truth."

Trying to vamp me. "How do you know?"

"Lot of people, when they lie, their eyes jump to the left a flicker."

"Get out."

"It's true."

"Mine didn't do that."

"You bet they did."

She laughed and lit her cigarette. Her eyes shut when she inhaled and she let the smoke rise slow from her mouth. Her voice came back low, almost pouty. "You said I needed money, right? I mean, we're agreed on that."

A twangy, forlorn tune climbed through the other voices and the jukebox shined pink and white through the smoke. "That's pretty low-down. No offense. You're real young. Seems like you might want to aim a little higher in career-type goals."

She stepped close and put her hand on my wrist. Dull, quickening heat traveled up my arm and across my shoulders. "I don't like it, man. But all my money's back in the city."

"You could have sold it but you overdid it. You shouldn't've put your hand on my wrist. It's too much." I hadn't pulled my hand away, though, and then she stepped back, her bottom lip falling and trembling a little.

I finished my JW. "It's no big deal. Just don't try to play me, girl. Down that road is nothing good for you."

She crossed her arms and gritted her teeth, started building herself a nice little fort of indignation, but I stopped her before she could speak. "Calm down. Just stop. Cut the baby-doll shit and the little halfway come-ons. Okay? And I won't bullshit you." I set down my bottle and her lips relaxed into a cute, confounded snarl. She tapped her foot. I said, "Look. I'm offering you something, and believe me when I tell you it is *way* more than most people get from me. I'm saying: be honest with me. You don't try to play me and I'll be straight with you. If I don't trust you, you can't come with me."

She hit the cigarette once, defiantly. "So you thought about it? We can hide out together?"

"Maybe. Only for a little while. Just be square with me."

"About what?"

"About who you are."

"Okay. You first." She stuck out her jaw and blew smoke, held the cigarette out from her face. "Who *are* you?"

I shrugged. "I'm what they call a bagman." I finished my Bud in a long swallow and put out my cigarette. "Also, I found out this morning that I'm dying of cancer."

"I think—wait. What did you say?"

"This morning."

"You—*really?*"

I bobbed my head. "You're the first person I told," I chuckled.

"Oh *God*. I'm *so* sorry, man. I had an aunt. Wait. Really? Are you *really* being for real with me?"

"Look at my face." She did. "My lungs are full of shit and I am going to die soon. I found out this morning."

"*Oh*. Man. I had an aunt with the cancer. It ate her up. She looked like gristle."

"I don't want to talk about it or anything. And I don't want you reminding me about it. You won't know me long enough to give a shit." I lit another cigarette and her eyes widened on it.

"Hey. Should you be—?"

I blew a smoke ring. "Why stop now?"

"Wow. Cheers to you, man."

A drunk with burn scars on his neck nodded lecherously between the two of us as he stumbled into the bathroom door. Rocky said, "You haven't . . . you have a girl or family or anybody? I mean, that you should *tell*?"

"No. What'd I just say about reminding me about it?"

"Sorry. Damn." She laughed softly to herself. Her face bloomed when she smiled, and her eyes creased and twinkled.

"What?" I said.

"This has really been one hell of a day for you, huh, man?"

"The hellest."

I thought about Sienkiewicz's house, the men in the foyer, Angelo's skull—but mostly about how fast I'd moved, how my thoughts and actions had flowed like quicksilver. As if certain death had burned away anything unnecessary, made me faster, more pure, the way it did for cowboys and swordsmen in movies I favored.

So even then in the bar with her I felt myself changing, becoming something different. She rattled the ice melting in her glass. "What do you want to do?" she asked.

I twisted my bottle on the rail, watched the perspiration slide. "How about we get drunk?"

"For sure."

I went back to the bar and returned with drinks, and she was alone, but the boys at the pool table still kept an eye on her.

We toasted. She said, "But then what? Next?"

I shrugged. "Tomorrow we go on." Nothing felt as risky as it was. As though I were protected, on a streak. I felt so sensory and aware I could almost detect each individual atom of smoke rolling over my skin like crushed gravel.

She sipped her drink and the ends of her lips curled, stamped two dimples on her cheeks, and in her smile flashed the danger of momentum, of riding hard with no plan.

But I didn't need a plan, only movement. Like the purest assassin, I was already dead.

People especially watched us when we left the bar, because nobody liked the idea of what it looked like we'd be doing next—a man like me and a girl like that. I was squinting through the windshield and Rocky's head kept nodding to her shoulders. I drove under the interstate where I knew a few hotels existed but they were all somehow too bright, and so I took us southeast to the black part of town, paid for a motel room looking out on an abandoned lot and boarded-up strip mall. A place called the Starliter. I paid cash, and the old woman behind the desk was nearly bald, dipping snuff, and she didn't ask for ID. She reminded me of Matilda, the woman who'd cooked at the group home, meals of blood pudding, powdered eggs.

The room had a single king-size bed and the A/C rattled the windowpanes. Rocky went to the bathroom while I pulled off my boots and stuffed my pistol down one, tucked them with the lockbox under the bed. I took off my jacket and belt and fell back on the room's only chair, my feet planted flat and my eyes closed to the ceiling, letting the spinning world resolve.

The bathroom door creaked and I opened my eyes a hair. She

walked out in her panties and a halter top, her short hair wet and slicked back. The bulb in the bathroom gave her the lighting of one of those classier-type centerfolds. She left her other clothes folded under her purse in a corner, and I kept my eyes slitted so it looked like I was dozing. She stood next to me and I could smell her, a musky, florid patch of atmosphere.

Her hand on my shoulder. "Roy?"

I opened my eyes. Her panties were light blue, the kind with string on their sides, and her hip bones jutted sharply out of them. I was staring level with the small cupped mound at the center of her legs. Her fingers moved real light on my shoulder. "You want to come to bed?"

"I'm fine here."

"It's okay. You can."

I sat up and blinked back cobwebs. Her downward face, fox-like, showed me moist, parted lips.

"Something else," I said. "What we talked about in the bar. About being straight. Don't be walking around in your panties in front of me or anything. I don't want you doing that."

"Why not?" she said, while her other hand slipped along her thigh and rubbed her flat stomach. "After what happened today? You don't like me?"

"I'm just telling you. Stop."

She stepped back toward the bed. "Okay." As she climbed into bed her ass jutted high, narrow and round and cleft as a peach, the kind just about every white man I know fantasizes to, including me, and the triangles of silk let the sides of her butt peek out, and there was nothing on her that wrinkled or jiggled. I don't know what was wrong with me. Getting drunk, I'd been thinking about Carmen, and about Loraine, wondering if she'd gotten a divorce, and Rocky was prettier than either of them, and like most men the idea of sex with a young woman implied a measure of immortality to me. But I just wasn't into the idea. She settled in the sheets while the air conditioner jangled and shook, the cold air going down into my chest.

She spoke quietly, without turning from the wall. "You can sleep up here if you want. You should sleep in bed. I won't do nothing."

She'd bundled the covers over herself. I rose and lowered myself on the bed, and the mattress creaked and sank. I lay flat on my back with my hands folded on my stomach. Her curled body inched just a bit closer to me, clenched and facing away.

I shut my eyes to the racket of the A/C and gradually felt her breathing settle into a deep, slow rhythm. In the dark I started thinking about that man whose apartment I'd visited earlier in the day, the one with betting slips and empty bottles and the picture of the woman and child. He wouldn't have to worry about seeing me now.

I wondered what he would do with his borrowed time.

I wondered if he would run.

In the morning Rocky snored gently beside me, the covers kicked off her four-alarm legs, the worn panties thin and clinging to her ass, one string fraying. I woke thinking about Mary-Anne. My mother had strawberry blond hair and a pretty, strong-boned face, a dramatic face, and when she didn't wear makeup she'd have dark raccoon rings, her only real flaw, but one that made her face deeper, and her eyes rummaged over things, searching out trinkets. She stepped out on John Cady a bit. It was obvious, and I later came to think he must not have minded.

Sometimes she'd stay home and listen to Hank Williams records with her hand on her chin at the kitchen table. Drinking rum punch until her eyes took on a blowsy, dazed character. Then she might want me to dance with her. I was always tall, and she could put her head on my shoulder and the clattering fan would blow the smells of her sweat and soap warmly over me, and the skin of her arms would stick to my neck a little.

Those nights she might tell me a story. Her stories were about the time before me, when she worked in Beaumont for a man

45

named Harper Robicheaux, who ran a nightclub. She liked to talk about him. He was a shot caller who'd been good to her, and she had stories of singing for people at the nightclub, wearing long spangled dresses and smoking with an ebony cigarette holder. Talking about it, she might start to sing, and she did have a rich, trembling voice that was almost too low and smoky for a woman. She'd sing things by Patsy Cline or Jean Shepherd, but when she'd stop singing the way she grinned was a sad sort of act that almost frightened me.

She never got right after John Cady fell off that cooling tower, and she started hanging out with people I didn't know.

Her body washed up on Rabbit Island, this empty patch of forest in the middle of Prien Lake, where the I-10 cantilevered over the waters.

When I woke these memories of Mary-Anne were close to the surface of me. Wet and dreary daylight sifted gray through the window of our room at the Starliter. I didn't feel at all like I had the night before. All that sureness and alignment with fortune seemed gone.

There was a broken promise in the room's cold walls. Old hopes bayed like ghost dogs inside me, just the old frustrations, old resentments, and I was pissed to find them at my heels this morning, tracking me across the years.

I got up to have a smoke and left Rocky curled on the bed. A snapped pine craned over the parking lot and marked the beginning of a weedy field that fell down into a shallow ravine full of broken bottles and burst garbage bags. The sun hadn't quite crested the horizon and a pearling light filled the sky, hauled shadows from the motel's flaking white paint, revealed a water stain that ran across the whole U-shaped building. Cracks mapped the pavement to its edges where the asphalt fractured into small chunks.

I deemed the weather offensive, the way the air lay on me like a giant tongue, clammy, warm and gritty as embers. I thought about Stan and Carmen, and I wondered if she'd known about what he tried to do to me.

I flicked my cigarette and went back inside.

The shower hissed from behind the door, and the empty bed was a tangle. I sat on the edge of it, squeezed my fists to stop the morning shakes.

She stepped out the door, wrapped from chest to thighs in a white towel; her slicked-back hair isolated her face as though a spotlight trained on it. "Hey," she said. "I'm putting clothes on now. I just gotta get them. I'm not trying nothing." A sheepish tone in her voice irritated me.

"What's that supposed to mean?"

"What?"

"You trying to say there's something wrong with me 'cause I don't want to fuck you?"

"No. No—"

"I'm leaving you here."

"*What?*"

"Enough of this baby-doll, come-hither bullshit."

"What's the matter with you, man?"

I stood up and she backed toward the bathroom, clothes in hand. "Stop it, man. You look like, like you looked at them boys last night."

"You're going to have to call somebody. I'll leave you a few bucks."

Her face was scared, and with her hair back it looked innocent, unimpeachable. I stared at my boots, opened and closed my fingers. "Look," she said, "I been thinking. A lot. About what you said last night. You're going to need somebody, Roy. I seen how sick people get."

"Shut up about that."

"All right. Look. But what you said last night. And then we get here and I do something like that. I'm real sorry about that. I don't know what it was. Just the drinking, I guess. The way you talked to me. But I appreciate it, Roy, the way you talked to me last night."

I glanced at myself in the mirror. My nostrils white, the lines in my forehead deep and drained of color.

"I wanted to tell you I really do appreciate it. Everything. Everything you did. You could of done anything you wanted with me, but you helped. When I was trying to get something over on you—I don't even *know* what. And you talked to me good. So I was thinking about that in there, Roy."

As she talked that dim pride from the previous night stirred in me, the heroic feeling, and she sat on the bed and drew her clothes to her chest. "I was thinking about you, too," she said. "What's happening to you. I don't mean to remind you. I *don't.* But, listen. I know you don't need me around, Roy. I *know* that. But I *think,* I mean the way things are, I think you *might.* Eventually. I think of maybe you having a friend to help you out, do things when you need it." She faced the wall and cinched the towel tighter. "I'm just saying, if it comes to that, and you need someone around. You want to play it straight, like you said— then I'd do it. I won't lie to you. I *can* pay my own way. And if anybody's looking for me, I have you to help me out. And if you get bad, or, *you know,* then you got *me* helping you out."

I opened my hands and gripped my knees, felt my face slacken. We were an unlikely pair in that hotel mirror. "All right, Rocky. We'll see how it goes. For a little while." I let my neck hang down and took a deep breath. "And start calling me John. That's my new name." My new papers said John Robicheaux.

"You can count on me, John." She rose and walked to the bathroom, stopped at the door. "And I can count on you."

First thing after leaving the Starliter I bought a *Times-Picayune* and a box of doughnuts at a Kroger's, and Rocky and I sat in the parking lot eating them with coffee while I looked through the paper.

I went through it front to back but there was no mention of any murders in Jefferson Heights, and when I thought more about it I realized the only sound had been the two blasts from my gun, and that might have been muffled enough by the old plaster walls to blend with the general city noise. Or maybe people had heard and no one cared. In either case, Stan would have cleaned the thing up.

"I never seen somebody put that much sugar in coffee. That was like half the cup," Rocky said.

I put my coffee on the dash and reached under the seat to the manila folder stuffed with papers. The blood on the pages was dry and rust-colored, and I opened it on top of the newspaper. Manifests. Records of lost cargo containers. Records of payment. A long, signed testimony by Sienkiewicz. The name Ptitko in cursive. *Ptitko* all over the place.

"What is that?" Rocky asked, stuffing her cheeks with bear claw.

I closed the folder, slipped it back under the seat. "I don't know yet."

I drove us to a Hibernia and emptied my bank account, another six hundred dollars to add to the three large. She was pretty thrilled to hold the bills in her hands. Her hair had dried to a bouncy blond fluff, almost punk rock.

An easy beauty to her. It was consoling in a way. The way a pretty face can be calming, like.

West on I-10. She found a tape of Patsy Cline and started singing softly along, and I almost asked her to stop because of what it called to mind, but I didn't. The land we passed split like a shattered clay tablet into grassy islands and all the dark, muddy water spread down to the Gulf in the southern distance. The sunlight glazed ripples and mud shallows with white fire.

We crossed Sulphur and the petroleum refineries, a kingdom of piping and concrete, noxious odors. She stopped singing and turned off the radio.

"Roy? Would you go ahead and take us to Orange? Like you said?"

"What? Why?" My voice almost cracked. "You want me to drop you off?"

She shook her head. "No. I meant what I told you this morning. Every word. But what I said about paying my own way. I can get some money."

"In Orange, Texas?"

"I can."

"How?"

She narrowed her eyes at the windshield and then turned to

look at the broken cypress trees that passed like brown bones reaching out the mud. "Don't worry about it. Somebody there owes me money. Go ahead and stop in Orange for a second."

"Now you *want* to go to Orange."

"We're on I-10 anyway. It don't make no difference."

"Who you going to see?"

"This dude there owes me money. I just thought of it this morning."

"You think he's just gonna pay you?"

"He'll pay me. I have *no* doubt about that."

Her voice had dropped a note and her stare had deep focus. I thought for a minute. "You're planning to have me talk to him, is that it? I'm supposed to get it for you. I'm like your muscle now?"

"No."

"*No?*"

"Nope. I don't need you to do anything except give me a ride."

I rolled it over in my head. "All right, then."

"Would you, if I asked?" she said. "If I'd asked you to get it for me, you think you would've?"

I squeezed the steering wheel, scowled at myself. "I might have."

"That's okay. I don't need you to do that. Thanks, though." The spindly shapes of bare, twisting trees were like brain stems, and the white herons roosting in one sprawled cypress seemed to follow the truck with their beaks. She kneaded the material of her purse. "I'm talking to him myself."

"That's safe?"

"Hell, yes, it's safe."

"You really want to take the chance? We got money. I mean, I didn't mean what I said before. You don't really need to be getting money right now. When we get where we're going we'll figure something out."

"No. It's okay. This is something I need to do. I made a promise." She watched the windows with a cold, practical reserve I hadn't yet seen on her.

"You want to tell me what the hell you're talking about?"

She rolled her head over on her shoulder. "I'll tell you if you ask, because I said I would. But I'd really rather you didn't ask."

A green sign said Orange was eight miles away. "All right," I nodded. "I guess."

She folded her fingers on her purse and sighed. All this rolling world of kudzu and bony trees and black water seemed to mean something to her, the way it meant things to me, and she watched out the window with a surrendering gaze. For both of us the landscape had a gravity that tugged us backward in time, possessed us with people we used to be.

We passed a small main street of shabby food joints, a gas station, credit union. High, wild grasses. She said, "The Tastee Freez. That's where we used to all go." But she wasn't really talking to me.

The flat prairie stabbed outward to the sky, crowded at the fringes with bushy trees, whiffs of ammonia and wet wood. The very air in these parts is so bright, it actually collects light, and you have to squint even when looking at the ground.

She guided me through a couple turns, and the neighborhoods were slight and set far back off the road, the houses ramshackle and shaded behind drooping oaks and willows. In this climate all things seek shade, and so a basic quality of the Deep South is that everything here is partially hidden.

She took us southwest and eventually into vine-clotted dells, past trailers scabbed with rust. Another gas station was fronted by broken foundation stones where the pumps had been ripped out, glassless windows, almost entirely overtaken by weeds and kudzu. We passed the school football field, and leaving the town proper, a black billboard posted off the road read in white letters HELL IS REAL.

Consumed by the boonies, having left even the sparsest trailer parks behind, she had me stop a few dozen yards down from a wooden cabin set beside a forest of tangled shrubs and grass that had been cooked the color of wheat by the sun. The cabin was about the size of a very old, poor hunting camp. A corroded water heater leaned against one wall, and one of those inflatable punching-bag clowns stood off in the high grass, its vinyl smeared with mildew. Brown vines overran the house, and one window had been stuffed with newspaper. A dead Chevrolet sat on blocks, overgrown as if the field were slowly digesting it, and a little tin shed bent sideways against the forest. The requisite torn screen door. The whole thing looked like the kind of place bikers keep to cook their meth.

We sat with the truck idling. The sun whitened the fields and all around was nothing but open, glowing air. She just squeezed the purse between her hands and stared at the little cabin as if she could crumble it with her eyes.

"You're sure about this?" I said. "Why don't I go in with you? I'll just stand there. Believe me, that's usually plenty."

"No. Thanks. There's nothing gonna hurt me in there." But she seemed to be speaking to someone outside the window. "It's better if it's just me."

"Suit yourself," I said, but she didn't move and we sat there another minute. The grass was so dry it crackled in the breeze. "Just holler if something happens," I added. "I'll come running."

She opened the door and stepped down. "Just give me like ten minutes."

"You sure this person's home?"

"'Course he's home. He don't go nowhere. People come to him if they want." She shut the door and walked carefully down the ditch with the purse under her arm, across the tousled yard, where flattened aluminum cans glittered in patches of lawn. The bright field made her look very small and alone, and her figure shrank as she neared the house. She followed the tree line and circled the cabin instead of using the front door, disappeared around the side. Animal twitters and a dry rustling scratched the silence.

I dug out the manila folder and opened it again. I guess Sienkiewicz thought all these papers were a safeguard or something. I pondered extortion angles. But it wouldn't really matter, because I couldn't blackmail or barter with what I had coming.

The house was still, no noise or sign of life, its wood bleached and weathered like the prairie around it.

A sharp, unmistakable pop echoed across space. A gunshot.

I looked around, and the dirt road was empty, rising into a hill behind me. It could have been somebody hunting squirrel or dove around here. Nothing moved from the house.

I jumped out the truck with my Colt in hand, vaulted the ditch, and jogged up the yard, but my boots slid in mud and I fell to my knees. Picked up the gun and ran wheezing, drenched with the heat. I was about halfway to the house when Rocky stepped out the front door. I tried to catch my breath, doubled over. When I rose up she was closer, and horror shot through me.

Rocky was leading a little girl toward the truck, a little blond girl.

I turned around and sprinted back to the Ford. She called behind me, "Roy! Roy, wait!"

"Wait yourself!" I yelled, pumping my legs, boots slipping on the slick grass. I slammed the truck door and the engine turned over a few times before starting, so I had to watch in panic as Rocky tried running through the field with a couple knapsacks, tugging the little girl behind her, shouting at me. They'd made it to the ditch when I hit the gas and sprayed pebbles and dirt fishtailing back on the road.

I overrevved and in the rearview the two of them were standing in the road, Rocky waving her hand as a mountain of brown dust swallowed them.

The road ahead was hard dirt and seemed to lead toward deeper woods, outright wilderness, possibly water. I tried to remember the last outpost of civilization we'd seen on the way to that house, how far they'd have to walk.

I started braking.

I told myself I'd ditch them. I'd cut them loose. But first I'd give her a ride, toss her some cash.

When I came back they were standing by the side of the road, the bags at their feet. Rocky's hands were on her hips, a fine layer of khaki dust powdering them. Her jaw jutted in her pissed-off way, but also like she'd known I'd come back.

She lifted the little girl up first, and the child had bold brownish green eyes that stared into mine longer than any adult's would be comfortable doing. She settled in the middle of the seat, watching me. "Um," I said.

"Who're you?" she asked.

"John."

The girl furrowed her brow. "No, you're not," she said.

"Tiff! Be nice." Rocky shut the door and brushed some dirty hair off her forehead. "This is Tiffany." The knapsacks sat on the floor between her legs and she held the purse with one hand, put her other arm around Tiffany, drawing her close. She turned up the A/C while the little girl appraised me. The girl smelled like a wet dog.

"It's going to be fine, Tiffy. We're going on a trip. Tiffinanny." She tickled the girl, and Tiffany giggled, but kept staring at me. Rocky looked between her and the windshield while I drove us back to the interstate.

I said, "Let me see your purse, Rocky."

"Why?"

"Hand it over now. Or I'll take it."

She blew bangs off her forehead, snapped up the purse, and tossed it on my lap. It was heavy.

I opened it and the pistol sat on top. It had belonged to one of the men with masks in Sienkiewicz's house. The silencer had been removed and lay on the bottom of the purse, under tissues and makeup. I guess I'd finally thought to wonder what she had taken off those men when she'd rifled their stuff. The gun was still warm.

I took all this as a massive betrayal. "What the hell, Rocky?"

"Watch your language, man."

"*My*—?" I pulled onto the shoulder. "You're playing a dangerous game with me, girl."

The little one glared up at both of us. Her cheeks were plump and soft, streaked with old dirt, and they trembled enough for me to modify my tone. She seemed too thin, and her hair was so blond it looked nearly white. Rocky just petted the girl's head and stared out the window. A sheriff's car passed us.

"This is my sister. She's coming with me. You can drop us off somewhere if you don't want her around, but she's coming with me."

The girl's nightie was the color of thunderclouds, and her skin had a luster of downy hair all over, and it made my skin look like adobe brick. "What's her daddy think about that?" I said. "What'd you do with that gun? What was that shot I heard?"

She snorted. "He's fine. I just scared him. So he'd know I could do it."

I put the truck in gear and moved back to the interstate. It began to fill with more cars. When she didn't say anything else, I said, "You shot at your stepfather."

"I shot at the *wall*. He got off lucky."

"Christ hell. You don't think he might be calling the cops?"

"He ain't calling the cops. He don't want the cops anywhere near that place."

"Jesus, what a stupid thing to do."

"I might rather you curse than the way you keep Christing this and Jesusing that. What're you so into Jesus for that you got to use His name like that?"

Another patrol car perched on an overpass and it seemed to observe us with the indifferent appetite of an owl.

"You don't think maybe you should of told me about this? That you were going to do this? What's that word we used— *straight*?"

"I'd of told you if you asked."

"You told me *not* to ask."

"And I really appreciate that you didn't."

"This is kidnapping. They're gonna be all over us." I'd put an absurd whisper into my voice.

Tiffany looked back and forth between us, but she didn't seem frightened anymore or especially put out to be here. Rocky said, "It's not kidnapping. He ain't gonna say nothing to anybody. He'll be glad. He'll still get the checks when they come."

I shook my head and kept checking the road and rearview for smokeys. Vans and cars and trucks and lots of eighteen-wheelers crowded the mirror; chrome trims glistened, tinted windows stared. "What do you imagine we're going to do with this?" I said. "I don't know what the play is here, Rocky. It doesn't make sense."

"Well, me and her are going to settle somewhere awhile. I'm going to get a job or something. I'm going to take care of her now. She'll almost be starting school soon."

"*School*? Are you—Christ."

She turned to me, stroking the girl's white hair. "You remember what I told you last night? About Vonda." Rocky nodded at her sister. "She's going to get a better deal." The little girl considered me too, and with such unmistakable suspicion that I took her to be fairly bright. Then the girl yawned and buried her face in Rocky's side.

"You know we're—what I'm saying. The things that might happen, from the people looking for us. Now you're making her part of that. Did you think about that?"

She didn't flinch from my eyes. "You're going to have to take my word for it when I tell you this's better than where she's coming from. And how's anybody going to find us? Cut your hair. I'll dye mine or something. And now we're *three* people. Who's looking for *three* people?"

My balls clenched when a patrol car crawled off the median. He got in front, though, and I let him move far ahead. "I'm giving you a ride. But you two are on your own. This isn't what we talked about."

"We can do anything we were going to do before. Only now I'll take care of Tiffany."

"You're making this sound real easy considering the way you were taking care of yourself up till today. Like you don't really know what you're talking about. Like you're just hoping and hoping that's what'll happen. And when it doesn't, the pavement's going to rush up and smack you."

Tiffany reached out and brushed the bristle ends of my beard. She looked at Rocky and said, "Like Santa?"

"Yes, baby. That's right, Tiffy. It's like Santa's."

The girl turned back to me. "You're not Santa."

This frustrated me more. "Did you even get any money?"

She frowned. "Not much. Gary had about eighty bucks on him and I took that. There was nothing left to even sell, really."

"Who's going to watch your sister while you work this supposed job?"

She licked her fingers and used the spit to wipe a smudge of dirt off one of her sister's cheeks. "Maybe I'll work somewhere that lets me bring her. Sometimes she'll be in school. Damn, man, the biggest morons in the world can raise kids."

I wrung my hands on the steering wheel. "Not well."

"You know," she said, "the more I think about it, the more I don't understand your complaint here."

I wanted to shout, but it dawned on me that all my objections involved the future, and I didn't really have one.

She said, "Remember what you said? Well, we're giving you

an *opportunity*, man. You don't need us now. I know. But you just might need us in your time to come."

Tiffany made a soft noise and nuzzled in to nap under Rocky's arm.

"I'm leaving you both."

"Fine," she said.

We were silent for a long stretch then with the wind shushing outside in the rhythm of a skier. A cloud-riddled heaven sealed the horizon, and I felt like we were bugs crawling along the edge of the world. Which we were, in a way.

I kept us westward, the sun at our backs, the girls' faces turning sleepy. That old rule came back. You do your own time, not someone else's. But what about after your own time is done, I wondered. I looked down at the little girl sleeping, one fist curled under her chin.

"Why'd you take the silencer off?" I asked.

Rocky shrugged and followed something out the window. "I thought it looked meaner without it."

I said, "You ever been to Galveston?"

She shook her head.

TWO

Certain experiences you can't survive, and afterward you don't fully exist, even if you failed to die. Everything that happened in May of 1987 is still happening, only now it's twenty years later, and what happened is just a story. In 2008, I'm walking my dog on the beach. Trying to. I can't walk fast or well.

I got a note this morning. Cecil wrote that a man is looking for me. Cecil owns the motel where I lease an efficiency unit and work as a handyman.

Right here and to the south the bronze fog in the morning appears endless, and the dusky color of it makes me think of sandstorms blowing in from far out in the Gulf waters, as if a desert sat beyond the horizon, and to watch the shrimp boats and jack-ups and supertankers materialize from it, you think you must be seeing another plane of existence breaking through to this one, and all of it freighted with history.

And the lesson of history, I think, is that until you die, you're basically inauthentic.

But I am still alive.

Sage runs circles around me, barking, but I don't move fast enough for her so I toss the stuffed giraffe out into the breaks and watch her leap after it. She bounces and plunges through the shallows, and I'm alone on the sand. The dawn ignites the fog and the soft sounds of birds honking and the low moan of ship horns mobilize the world. September, middle of hurricane season, the skies are coiled, lead-colored clouds that resemble spun sugar.

2008.

What an impossible year.

My left foot bends out as if it's always trying to walk away from me. I drag crooked tracks. The sand in Galveston is coarse and gray, specked with orange and yellow particles, and in the early morning the beaches are mostly deserted, and Sage runs freely up and down the shore with the gnarled giraffe in her mouth. I pass my tongue along the porcelain bridgework against my gums, and I remember.

The note Cecil left on my door is a small Post-It, and its message crashes through my mind like a rogue wave: *Roy—some hard-ass in a suit asking about you. Didn't give me a name.*

I guess I could get back to my room and start packing, light out for new territory a little farther west. It doesn't seem possible that they'd be looking for me now, but there's nobody else it could be.

Maybe twenty years later some goombah opens the books and gets the idea to settle old business. Maybe.

I ponder my history and admit that nobody looking for me could have friendly intentions. My stomach's heavy with this sense of a marker come due.

And the note has me thinking about Rocky even more than usual.

I think of her talking about herself in a bar in Angleton while green and purple lights from the dance floor glide through the sheen of her eyes, and her face grows more vivid when I remember that face as it told me things.

She talked about being four or five and sleeping in the backseat of a car in the woods, where a man had driven her mother. There were lots of trucks parked around a couple trailers, and her mother didn't come back till the morning, when she exited a trailer with her makeup smeared, and the man drove them both back home, and no one said a word.

Sage runs to my feet and rattles water off her coat.

I climb down the inlet beside the abandoned pier where I keep crab traps. My legs are stiff and the wet air causes my hands to ache and clench into claws. When I pay for things people notice my hands. The fingers are crooked and my knuckles bubble like blisters.

I could run, make a break for it.

But the solace of walking Sage and collecting the crab traps is a little thing I can allow myself this morning.

These are the same beaches where Cabeza de Vaca's men were reduced to cannibalism, where the pirates Aury, Mina, and Lafitte slipped the law. Here Lafitte, who built a fortress named Campeche, ran slaves, whores, saloons, and served as the island's governor until he had to flee after firing on an American vessel. But before his flight he treated the island to a four-day orgy overstocked with whiskey and women. Walking the foggy beaches in the morning, air thick with salt and decay, you get the impression this place is still nursing a hangover from all that history.

I think of Rocky holding my hand and telling me about being in that car as a little kid, and how it is the same thing with the history of this island. The stories have become the place. I read a writer who said that stories save us, but of course that's bullshit. They don't.

But stories do save *something*.

And they killed a lot of time for me over the last twenty years. More than half of them in prison.

Farther out, the gray cypress of the pier has rotted and the boards are broken and collapse into the brassy fog. A few gulls perch on the posts near the end of the thing, their chests out like tiny presidents. Fiddler crabs scuttle away from my feet. The calm, rhythmic slap of the tide. You can see the winds building farther out in the Gulf—the sky beginning to stir in a very slow, sweeping churn. The weather makes the bolts in my skull seem to tighten.

I stand under the dock, and the way the pilings converge at its center the pier looks like a flooded cathedral. I wince, closing my fingers around the line, and hoist up the wire cage, foamy film washing my tennis shoes. I flip the catch and dump four blue crabs into the canvas sack slung from my shoulder, then hinge the catch again and toss the basket into the tide. The crabs struggle and thrust against the bag, the heavy canvas stretching, and I realize I'm thinking about Carmen, too, this morning. I can almost taste that smell of Camel menthols and Charlie perfume instead of this salt-clotted air.

Climbing back up, I pause with Sage because past the broken pier, just outside the bank of bright fog, I see a school of bottlenose dolphin break the surface in greased arcs. Sage drops her toy at my feet and shakes water off again. The dog has a curious, flirtatious spirit, a red-and-white Australian shepherd, slim, with pale green eyes and a flopping tongue. We stand there a minute because I hope to see the dolphins again, but I don't. Bramble and thistle crust the dunes, and a barge crawls out the fog toward the shipping canals, slides across my good eye.

I wonder why Cecil referred to the guy as a "hard-ass." I wonder what questions, exactly, this man asked about me.

I could run.

Or I could stay put and wait. Face the music, as people say.

It strikes me that this might be a good death. And long overdue. Then the rise in my pulse and the speed of my thoughts turn into a sensation of careful, total awareness, like waking up.

I toss Sage's toy ahead and I turn to look at my crooked prints. The way my back and neck hunch you wouldn't believe I once stood six-three, and the patch on my left eye lends me a superficial resemblance to the pirates who once ruled this coast.

My shadow ahead is twisted enough to be some spindly, crustaceous thing that crawled from the tide. Shambling out of history.

fter I empty the crab traps I walk Sage through a couple parking lots to the doughnut shop. The air in Finest Donuts is as tense as I am. Roger hardly scratches Sage, and then only after she nuzzles his leg persistently. He stares at the chessboard and then at Deacon's face, which is slack-jawed, his eyes hooded, his long arms dangling, so black he looks like polished Shinola. Deacon hasn't been around the past couple days and now here he is, crack of dawn, and I can smell the gin and piss from the door.

Finest Donuts leases the last slot on the western end of a very small strip mall that's blocked from Seawall Boulevard and the beaches by another, much larger and newer strip mall to the south. The pizza place beside Finest closed months ago, so now there's only a locally owned drugstore and tobacco shop, and most days the strip's windblown parking lot is occupied only by sand drifts and discarded flyers. We just had the seventh anniversary of 9–11, and a small banner outside the store reads WE WILL NEVER FORGET.

I suppose that's one of the things we do in here. We sit around not forgetting.

"And now you have to start all over," Roger says to Deacon. "From zero. You give back the chip. You feel like it was worth it?"

I glance at Errol, who's at the counter blowing steam off his coffee, and he raises his eyebrows like it's been touchy in here all morning. One of the three pots of coffee is already emptied, and the ashtrays have a fair share of butts, so I wonder how long they've been up. The chess game looks like it stalled, with Roger having a tidy collection of Deacon's pieces.

"You begin by admitting you are powerless," Roger says to him, lighting a new cigarette. He chases the first drag with black coffee and folds his thick arms on the table. Roger keeps a small mustache trimmed to military regulations, and the ease with which his face communicates disappointment can feel a little tyrannical. I don't envy Deacon, whose eyes are lacquered and stunned, and I step over to Errol and lay my sack of crabs on the counter.

Roger says to Deacon, "You begin again. Over and over. Each time, whatever it takes." Deacon nods slowly, a tear scrawling down his cheek. He raises his cup of coffee with two hands, brings it to his lips slowly, like sacramental wine, and his look of confusion and shame reminds me of Rocky.

Deacon's bent neck reflects in the glass display facing the front of the store, a penitent shadow over the rows of doughnuts and cakes under fluorescent tubes. I think about Cecil's note, the man who's asking questions, and I wonder if they've sent more than one man to find me. I would.

Errol shakes his head, folds up a paper he'd had open to the racing form. "I won't go back to offtrack," he says to me. "You can't meet any woman worth a damn there, anyway." I sit down at a booth between him and the chess table, and Sage draws figure eights around my ankles before settling between my feet. Deacon nods at me and tries to smile. I notice he has a fresh knot of purple bruise on his forehead and a red stain in the white of one eye. He grew up here and blew a basketball scholarship to Texas Tech, and he was working as something at Wal-Mart, but the sense this morning is that's no longer the case. He calls me Captain Morgan sometimes, because of the eye patch.

"How you, Deacon?" I say.

"All right, all right." He blows on his mug. The smell of gin off him overpowers the coffee and pastries and even cigarettes now.

We're all on the program here, though really I don't have a choice—I can't drink, meetings or not, but I still come for the stories. And it gets me out of the apartment.

Roger checks his watch and says, "Why don't we start?" He goes through the twelve steps, asks if anybody wants to share. All eyes are on Deacon. He starts to speak but puts a fist to his mouth, shakes his head. Another tear skips helplessly down his cheek and he says, "I don't know if, right now, I mean—"

I want to help him out, and I sigh, "I'll share." This surprises everyone a little. Roger and Errol watch me closely. "My name's Roy. I'm an alcoholic. I got nineteen-plus years sobriety." They all say hi to me like we're meeting for the first time, and I look at Deacon. "You remind me of someone this morning. A girl I knew a long time ago. I guess I'm thinking about her a lot today. She had a hard life."

The canvas sack on the counter shifts and stirs. We come here to tell stories so that we can manage the past without being swallowed by it. They wait for me to go on.

"I'm thinking about her now. Something happened—I got a

note, this morning. It made me think about her." For one second I think I'm finally going to tell the whole thing, but I stop myself. Everyone's waiting for me to continue, though, and I end up just talking a little about Rocky.

She told me she had a long walk home from where the school bus stopped, and she had to walk under an old overpass that was filled with strange graffiti, and on the other end of the tunnel sometimes older boys hung out drinking and smoking, and when that was the case she'd have to wait in the darkness of the overpass, wait until they'd gone and the light at the end of the shaft was empty. Once she waited until after midnight, and when she got home nobody noticed she was late. Thirteen years old.

I stammer and mumble through the anecdote, and everybody looks confused when I'm done, but they thank me. It's obviously one of those stories that no one knows how to take. They can't understand the point.

The point of the story is how she told it, the way her face looked away when talking, glancing back to see if I was listening. The slow, measured quality of her words.

I know that for all of us here, the Finest Donuts chapter of AA, our testimonies let us bale up memory, bind years of degradation and guilt into these manageable units that we can put on a shelf, take down, and skim in the safety of tales.

I never told my real story.

Errol talks about losing a bunch of money at the track over the weekend. We thank him.

Deacon finally gets up the courage to tell us about the old friend he ran into at work, who offered to buy him a drink, and when he's done confessing and wipes his eyes, we thank him.

When we're done everyone stands for more coffee and I remember the book in my jacket. I take out a slim paperback, and I hand it to Roger. A novel I'd borrowed about two boxers in Southern California.

The book seems to interest Deacon, because he slides it off the table and starts reading the back cover. Roger huffs.

When he's dusted to the elbows with flour and sugar, you can't see the marine tattoo on Roger's left forearm, but right now it's a blurred greenish blue smudge beneath a canopy of thick hair, shaped vaguely like an anchor.

Errol says, "I'm saying we need to make a plan to meet *pussy*. You got to put yourself in the game. Who's with me?"

Deacon holds the book up to Roger and asks, "What you say this about?"

Roger says, "Fighting."

Errol shakes his head and cocks the brim of his trucker's cap down, snaps open his paper. Errol appeared at the meetings shortly after me, walking out the sand flats talking about how he'd been hauling rig across vast deserts and no-man's-lands, ice trucking in Canada, breaking highway up and down the Southwest. He chews his fingernails even when he doesn't want to, when he's talking to you, and his eyes will dart down and ask you to excuse the weakness of the habit. I've seen his rig but I don't know the last time he hauled anything in it.

Errol closes his paper again and says, "You need to project an aura of safety, of friendliness. Above all, they need to feel you're listening to them, even when there's no sense in it."

Roger says, "I think, at a certain point, you prefer to be lonely."

Roger has three ex-wives and bought the doughnut shop on the tail end of his last bender, in '92. He and Errol start talking about the new hurricane that formed off Cuba weeks ago and has been dancing up the Mexican coastline. Every other one gets a guy's name now, and this one's Ivan or Izzy or something.

"Gonna be bad."

"Might not."

"You seen what it looks like on the news?"

Then Leon pushes through the glass door and the bells jingle. "Sorry I'm late," he says. "Who owes alimony in here?"

"Flip the sign, would you?" Roger asks, and Leon turns around to spin the sign on the door to OPEN. When he turns back Roger says to him, "Thought your ex got married."

"Not me. One of you boys looks like you're getting served."

"What?" Errol says.

Leon leans against the doughnut counter and stretches his legs, enjoying the moment of withheld information. "Dude out there's watching the store. Parked across the lot. Saw him I's coming up the road."

I hoist myself up and Sage follows me to the window.

"Guilty conscience," Leon says, nodding at me.

Out the window I see at the back, far end of the lot, a black Jaguar sitting alone. There's a man inside wearing sunglasses and clearly watching the place. There's nothing else to watch this time of morning.

"What is it?" Roger asks.

I back away from the window. "He's right. Guy's watching the place." I move to the counter and take up my crab bag.

"What's with you?" Leon says.

"Nothing. Have to cut out early," I tell him. "Painting the boss's rental today." I click my tongue for Sage. She picks her toy off the linoleum and wags her tail at my ankles.

They're all watching me now.

"Hurricane might hit the next few days," Errol says, "and he wants to paint his house?"

I shrug and move past the counter and through the kitchen, my head throbbing, Cecil's note burning in my thoughts.

"Where you going?" Roger says.

I'm already walking at a trot, through the swinging door, and I call behind me, "Going out the back way."

When I push through to the alley behind Finest Donuts my heart's thrumming and I start trudging up the levee of sand that separates the next business park. My breath wheezes in the warm air. I think of hobbling out of Stan's Place twenty years ago, running through the field with shouts swelling behind me, gagging on my own tongue. I can tell myself I have no reason to assume that man in the Jaguar is following me, but I'm still afraid to look over my shoulder.

I haven't decided how to answer this paranoia. To stay or to run.

Rocky makes me want to stay.

THREE

Clear of the cities, Texas turned into a green desert meant to hammer you with vastness, a mortar filled with sky. The girls eyed it like a fireworks show.

The 45 causeway southbound, into the north side of the island: rainbow-colored sailboats stuffed the harbors, fishing trawlers whose nets draped from jibs like cypress moss. Bums crouched in the shade of palm trees and telephone poles. The palm trees were shorn of leaves and looked like gnawed ribs plunged into the dirt. A bony dog with matted fur limped down the sidewalk at a trot, maybe on his way to Pelican Island. Teenage girls in skimpy two-pieces, sitting on the hoods of cars, the sun in their teeth, in the chrome trim, the sun in the bottle caps strewn around the tires and the crushed beer cans stamped into the asphalt. The older guys crowded around them, passing out cans of High Life or Lone Star.

The Gulf was dark blue and dappled with napalm by the miles-wide sun that peered over it. The air had a coating that magnified the sun, shunting it into blades. All the people had coins in their sunglasses.

Girls in bikinis roller-skated along the seawall promenade, a group of skateboarders clanged and ricocheted off guardrails and curbs. Beach balls flew and bounced in the shadows of the big resorts along the shoreline. You could smell the open-air fishmarkets, the baskets of shrimp and peppered crawfish boils where the old beach dogs scrounged around for guts and shells under the tables.

Signs of history: old Spanish churches hardening in the heat; white stone and pink brick, adobe, stucco; a three-masted ship from the 1800s, full of false pride at the Seaport Museum.

You could broker the future here. Dump your memories into the white light of the Gulf like leaves into a bonfire.

The little girl's hands were on the window, her mouth hanging open. She whispered as if it were a secret. "What's it?"

Rocky spoke in her ear. "That's the ocean, baby."

"What's it?"

"Water, sweetheart. Lots and lots of water."

The brown beaches were strewn with washed-up gulfweed in a ragged line along the tide break. Rocky watched people who stood over smoking grills, and she watched the mostly naked girls and the boys following them like starving dogs. I could tell she was thinking about other lives. A lot of people her age expected to live forever and saw life as a kind of birthright to endless good times.

I never did see things that way, and I knew that she hadn't, either.

Now and then she looked harassed by her own potential, like certain young people, and you might notice then the way a stillness spread through her eyes, and her unguarded face forgot to play a role, just looked stunned by confusion and remorse, while the features of this face were organized by a kind of country pride that wouldn't admit confusion or remorse. I knew something about that, too.

I didn't know what to do with her.

I didn't quite understand why I was here, and I knew I wouldn't stay.

A reasonable and even kind course of action was to get a hotel for them, pay it up for a few days, and split. It was hard, though, to look at the little one and not feel some twinge of larger generosity. But that's the urge that fucks you, gets you paying tickets that aren't yours.

Middle-aged men lugged surfboards under their arms. Tour buses lurched like drunks around corners.

The place was different when I came here with Loraine, less developed. We'd rented a house on stilts along the beach, and it seemed more like a small town then. We'd grilled shrimp with beer batter and toasted tequila. Smoked pot together in the bathtub. She said we were best when we weren't serious, that there was no point in getting serious. I guess I never really believed her. Loraine once told me marriage was a social construct that turned pleasure into a business arrangement, and I tried to be cool about that. She was a lot younger than me, nine years. She made me feel like trying a straight life, though, welding or something, trying to settle down with her, but she would say, Does that pay as much? and, Why screw up a good thing?

I had wondered sometimes what that would have been like. Home in the evening, dinners. Having a couple tykes, watching them grow. I thought now that I wouldn't have minded trying that, giving it a whirl.

Both the girls just stared out the windows, and now and then the little one would gasp and dart her face to Rocky and point.

We drove all the way west along the seawall and then back, and they looked at the same things twice with fresh enthusiasm. I was trying to locate the place where we'd rented that house so many years earlier, but I think a stone-and-glass resort was there now. Or maybe I just couldn't find it.

I picked a motel a few blocks north of a pocket beach on FM 3005. It was L-shaped, its center a parking lot ruptured by thick shoots of scouring rush and weeds. Its walls were old brick painted baby blue, a single story with a flat roof and the low arm of the L jutting out into a glass office beside an old carport shaped like a painter's palette. A sign said WEEKLY RATES under a larger, vertical sign whose stacked letters read EMERALD SHORES. Outside the lot and near the street a stripped palm tree curved toward the ground, bent over a pile of yellowed fronds.

I turned off the truck and said to Rocky, "You all are my nieces, yeah?"

She nodded. "You're my mother's brother."

"Where's she now?"

She thought. "Vegas."

"Where's your father?"

She shrugged. "Died on an offshore rig. A cable knocked him overboard. I knew somebody like that."

The parking lot was empty except for a couple cars with bent antennas and rusted trim, a station wagon on two spares, a motorcycle propped over a dark pool of oil. Aluminum foil covered one set of windows. It was the sort of place for people with nowhere else to go, a motel where the occasional guest checked in to commit suicide, people too absorbed in their own failures to pay much attention to us.

I held open the door to the office for the girls. Three small fans focused around the counter and their hum mingled with the grinding roar of a boxy A/C wedged in a hole in the wall. Rocky held her sister's hand and they looked at a display stocked with tourist brochures.

I could hear a radio or television playing from a side room, someone ranting about liberals, and I rang the tarnished bell on the counter.

Tiffany kept rotating her head, staring at everything, the dimpled ceiling, the faded seashell wallpaper, the hard-stamped pink carpet. I bet the air-conditioning was something else for her.

A woman emerged out the room behind the counter, her flesh so grooved and dehydrated it might have been cured in a smokehouse. It was sun-baked the color of golden oak and draped across jagged bones. Squirrel gray hair. Her eyeglasses had a square of duct tape holding them together at the center, and she pushed them up on her nose.

"Help you?"

She looked over my shoulder at the girls. The two hard creases framing her mouth seemed like they reached down to the bone.

A piece of paper taped to the wall outlined prices, said the weekly rate for a single was one-fifty.

"We'll take two singles," I said. "Each for one week."

She cocked her head. "They're yours?"

"My sister's. Nieces."

"Well, that's a darling girl."

Rocky walked up and told Tiffany to say hi, but the little girl ducked behind her sister's legs, embarrassed.

"What's your name, precious?"

"Tell her your name, sweetie."

The girl laughed a little.

"It's Tiffany," said Rocky.

"How old is she?"

"Three and a half."

The woman's smile caused her face to rupture. I kept wondering what she'd looked like before the sun had its way with her.

We could hear the radio from the next room. I knew it was a radio now because the voices were those of a call-in talk show, and a man was discussing the New World Order and the Mark of the Beast. A starfish clock on the wall had stopped at eleven twenty.

She asked to see my driver's license and I slid the fake over with two hundreds and five twenty-dollar bills.

"There's another 24.67 for tax."

I gave her two more twenties and watched her fill out the card. Her hand shook when she worked the pencil and she seemed to have one ear turned toward the voices from the radio.

"I suppose we'll be all right," she said, cocking her head to the other room. "Being the sovereign state of Texas. The UN invades, we'd be the ones to shoot back."

I tried to smile but the face I made caused her to frown a little.

I said, "We're from Louisiana."

"Well." She returned to writing on the receipt. "Louisiana belongs to the Catholics."

I glanced at Rocky and told the woman, "All right."

She handed me a receipt with two room keys, each on a rubber surfboard.

"That's nineteen and twenty, right outside, directly across the lot. I'm Nancy Covington. You need something, I'm always here."

I thanked her but a further point seemed conveyed by her expression.

"Just to say," she added. "I'm good friends with lots of policemen. Just to say. Mind what goes on in the rooms."

Rocky and I looked back and forth and both girls smiled at the woman.

"Good *Lord*, that is an adorable girl. You must be the very cutest thing ever came through here."

"Let's hope she stays that way," said Rocky, and they both tittered.

Our rooms were side by side and each had dark green, all-weather carpet, oil paintings of the beach, and an imitation-wood dresser, nightstand, and small table. They smelled of suntan lotion, sweat. The wallpaper was the same peach-colored pattern of seashells as in the office, and in my room it was splitting at the seams and curling in the humidity. The sink faucet shook and rattled for a while when turned on, and maroon water stains painted the corners. Big A/Cs were stuck in holes under the window of each room, and the curtains were thick, navy blue, and their plastic coating blocked the sun like a wall of bricks. There was even cable TV.

Tiffany sat on their bed and soon got absorbed in a show with puppets and cardboard sets. I watched Rocky unpack their knapsacks and stow her sister's clothes in the dresser drawers. Her skirt hugged her ass when she squatted, and I felt my blood stir and cheer in admiration of it.

But there was still this kind of phony aspect to our scene. Like we were both pretending about something, and we weren't going to talk about it.

"What now?" she asked.

I thought a moment. "Suppose we should do some shopping."

"Um."

"Don't worry about it," I said. "I got it covered."

A dull warning prickled in me—old alarms raised by favors, the encouragement of certain dependencies.

"You shouldn't be paying for us, Roy."

"Not like I can take it with me."

I couldn't seem to stop myself. I wanted a drink pretty bad, too; I suppose to help me ignore those instincts that told me to hold on to my wallet and stop this playacting. Leave them *now*.

We found a JCPenney in a mall, and I waited while she chose some clothes. Malls make me edgy, people trying so hard to buy things, and it seemed like I noticed more and more fat people every day.

I watched Rocky hold up a skirt and blouse next to each other, and big women waddled among the racks, sifting hangers, checking tags, leaving pants unfolded and lying across displays, and they looked bloated and unhappy and hungry to spend.

I've found that all weak people share a basic obsession—they fixate on the idea of satisfaction. Anywhere you go men and women are like crows drawn by shiny objects. For some folks, the shiny objects are other people, and you'd be better off developing a drug habit.

Something becomes too enjoyable, too consistent, and before you know it, you're compromised.

This was what happened with Loraine, and I guess it had happened a little with Carmen, too. I resented that.

Rocky picked out a skirt, blouse, and two-piece swimsuit, and when I encouraged her she went back for a couple tank tops and a pair of jeans. At a K&B drugstore we bought toothbrushes and such, and I also bought a set of electric clippers. We went for lunch at a place near the hotel, close to the seawall, scoured wood with its own concrete tidewall, a mural of faded sea creatures painted across it. We ate on a patio and a group of teenagers congregated against the mural, smoking and posing, and Rocky hunched her shoulders a bit, pointed her face away from them. She took only a couple bites of her cheeseburger.

Tiffany ate her fries in a dainty manner, and Rocky looked between her sister and the teenagers, and it seemed like she didn't want to watch them but couldn't help it. She moved her food around, glanced at the kids, then dragged patterns in her ketchup with a soggy fry.

I washed down two burgers with a Budweiser, reclined a little, and inhaled the hot, salty air, stowed it in my lungs. "What do you think?" I asked her.

"Huh?" She dropped her fry. "I mean, thanks."

"What do you think about it here? It looks all right."

"It's okay."

"I bet she's gonna like the beach."

"Yeah." She crossed her arms on the table and looked down at Tiffany, and her smile struck stiff and quick.

"I bet you can get some kind of waitress job around here. You're cute. They'll hire you."

"Maybe."

A waiter in baggy shorts took our plates and asked Rocky if she wanted hers to go. She told him no but I said to wrap it. He walked off and she barely lifted her face, shifted the waxy place mat around.

I scanned the walls, fishing nets strung along the outside

and plastic crabs and crawfish stuck in the webbing, a marlin mounted above the doorway, framed newspaper articles about the 1900 hurricane. The past keeps revealing itself here. Surfaces are always eroding.

"What's wrong with you?" I said.

She looked hurt. "What do you mean?"

"You're sulking."

"I don't know. I mean, it just catches up to me sometimes." Her eyes gleamed when she said it. "I mean, I was doing all right, not thinking too much. It's just everything. You know."

"Right."

"Just. Everything since last night."

"We'll be fine. Nobody's going to find us."

Tiffany's head darted up and she shot a finger at my beard. "I *found* you!"

Rocky said to me, "I know. I think you're right, I mean. It's just the way things *are*. Now and then I think. It doesn't seem fair." She wiped her eye and chewed the back of her lip. "I just wonder if I can ever expect different."

I thought about her problem and pulled a cigarette, tamped it on the table, and said, "It doesn't seem fair, because it's random. But that's why it's fair. You get me? It's fair like a lottery's fair."

"Shit, Roy. Is that supposed to help?"

I lit my cigarette and pushed back from the table so I could stretch my legs. "Yeah," I said.

"Not for me." Her cheeks and nose flushed bright red, and she blinked back tears.

"Look, though. It works both ways. Tomorrow you could get rich and fall in love." I'd never believed that, but I tried to sound convincing.

"Oh, yeah. I'm sure."

She started folding and unfolding her place mat and looked past the levee toward the ocean. She seemed especially small, too young and frail against the backdrop of long red cloud strands and golden sky. I watched Tiffany drawing in her ketchup with her fingers. She looked up at me and then at her messy hands and she laughed, sucked her fingers clean, and poked them back in the ketchup.

On the way home I bought a paper so Rocky could look through the classifieds. I wanted her to begin having thoughts about the future again, mostly because I thought that would make it easier to leave them. Tiffany started nodding off as soon as we were back at the motel, and Rocky's eyelids fluttered, a rapid exhaustion taken hold, so we split up at our rooms.

An empty six-pack container stood next to the curb as though waiting for a bus. Across the parking lot a shirtless man was sitting on the stoop outside a room, his head in his hands.

I shut my door. Before I plugged in the clippers I took my knife and hacked off the pelt of hair at the back of my head. I held it in my hand a moment because I was a little surprised how long it was, and I kind of felt like I'd lost a part of myself more crucial than I'd supposed. Then I dropped it in the trash and turned on the clippers. I put a quarter-inch guard on and shaved my head and used the same setting on my beard, so that my jaw and scalp had an even level of gray-blond stubble.

I confronted my face. My reflection was always what I knew it would be and never quite what I expected, but this time it was brutal—the large planes of empty flesh, the small bent nose, the slit of mouth and wide, squared chin. My whole life it seemed I'd dimly anticipated seeing another face besides this severe mask Loraine once compared to the features on a Choctaw totem pole. The comparison was true when I was young, and more true now with a longer brow, my hair retreating in a widow's peak, my eyes drooped and cheeks falling. The eyes were odd to me. Dark brown, widely spaced, they seemed larger without all the hair. But as long as I could remember, it seemed like my real face went unrepresented, that there was within me another face, with sleeker, purer features, a sharp jaw and Roman nose, the bust of some centurion who conquered the ancient world. Forty years now with the same face, and still a part of me expected to see the other guy in the mirror.

I ran my hand over my bristly scalp and thought of chemotherapy patients.

I left the television off and stretched out on the bed. Water stains blotched the ceiling like tiny continents no one had ever charted, and I imagined algae blooming throughout my chest in a chain of eruptions.

I wondered how bad this was going to get, and I wondered how I would handle it when it got bad.

I had put my Colt and the gun Rocky took in the lockbox, along with the money, and I kept it at the bottom of my duffel bag. The bullet train had more appeal than getting sick, but the problem with suicide is that by the time anybody goes through with it, the damage is already done. And to be honest it frightened me, though in my time I'd done lots of things that scared me.

Drinking myself to death in Mexico also held some attraction.

But in either case the irony pestered me. I was the one left standing in that foyer. Why should the only man to walk out that house be the one who was planning on dying anyway?

Weirdest, I had no real urge toward revenge. Which is not like me at all.

There was even, I think, some part of me glad to be done with it all, with the gamblers and junkies and Stan Ptitko and the Armenians, and it could be I'd been feeling this way for a while, which was the real reason I'd gotten that other identity made up in the first place.

I was *out*.

Beyond the room the insects chirred and the world began to stain darker, reds and blues seeping between the curtains, colors that recalled a street corner in Hot Springs, years ago, and the bugs and the faint shushing of the ocean joined the noise from the air conditioner. A woman's voice skittered from the other side of the window, laughing, and I heard someone stumble and a bottle broke.

I closed my eyes and there was Carmen, smiling over her shoulder. Loraine clawing at my sides. I remembered that at the street corner in Hot Springs with the red and blue lights, the lights were in a puddle and I had been sitting on a curb like the man out in the parking lot. My knees bent and my head between them, my knuckles bloodied.

My stint in reform school: heating a toothbrush under a book of matches till I could twist off the bristles and shove a razor blade into the soft plastic.

When I was seventeen and bar-backing at Robicheaux's, a tiny old man drank quietly all night by himself once, didn't talk to anybody, and around midnight I saw him fall off his stool. Cracked his head open and died right there at everyone's feet.

I opened my eyes.

Things can't hold up here. The salt gets into everything, stripping paint, rusting fenders, corroding walls. I could smell the room thick with it, and in the water stains on the ceiling I saw cities and fields of erosion.

You're here because it's somewhere. Dogs pant in the streets. Beer won't stay cold. The last new song you liked came out a long, long time ago, and the radio never plays it anymore.

A shy knock sounded on my door, and I rolled to my feet. Rocky stood in cold sodium light, wearing a T-shirt and a pair of little blue shorts fixed all the way up her legs. She was hugging herself and a blush saddled her nose and cheeks, her eyes chafed.

"Roy."

She came inside and I shut the door, turned on the lamp. I sat across from her on the bed. She drew her knees up and curled her legs in the chair, and I couldn't stand the view it afforded, so I had to be careful to place my eyes just to the side of her. She sniffled and hugged her knees.

"What's wrong?"

"Look at you. All your hair's gone."

"What happened?"

"Nothing. I been thinking."

"A late bloomer."

"Right." She chuckled and sniffled and brushed a blond lock off her forehead. "I's just thinking. I think—how old are you?"

"Forty."

"I mean, I'm *eighteen*, man. That's nothing. Right? I mean, no matter what happened up till now."

"Eighteen *is* nothing. You got time to start your life over three or four times if you want."

When I said that to her was the first time I really felt too young to die. The dumbest complaint. I thought how everybody says the same thing when I come to see them with my gloves on and my baton out. *Wait, wait,* they say. Wait.

Her eyes were wet and she'd rubbed her nose raw. She faced the window, where harp strings of light drew around the curtains, and her eyes focused on something beyond them. "Talk to me, Roy. I need to hear something, man."

I didn't say anything. I couldn't stop glancing at her legs and thighs. Desire always seems vaguely humiliating.

"What were you doing when you were eighteen, Roy?"

I took out a cigarette and offered her one. I lit them both. I said, "I was working in a bar and running playback bets around the south, Louisiana and Arkansas and Mississippi, mostly."

"What's that?"

"It's where you put money on horses to juke the odds for bookmakers."

"Oh."

More sounds drifted from outside, and our smoke unspooled and broke against the discolored islands on the ceiling. Music from car radios a block away, a woman down the sidewalk shouting to a man about *re-spon-si-bil-i-ties*, really snapping off each syllable.

"How'd you get into doing that?" Rocky asked.

I shrugged. "I was supposed to join the Marines."

"Oh, yeah?" She folded her legs down across her and straightened her face to mine. Her nose and cheeks were bandaged by pale blond freckles, and the moisture made her eyes look wider. "What do you mean?"

"When I turned seventeen, I took the bus to go to the recruiting center. I did. I sat in there a couple hours. There were a lot of boys in there. They had their mothers or fathers with them, and they wore jeans as patchy as mine. Mended shirts. Their hands were real calloused from farmwork. The mothers and fathers couldn't scrub all the dirt off themselves. I watched the men doing the recruiting, talking to the parents. That was what they did. They hardly talked to the boys. They just told the parents, *We'll teach him this, he'll learn that, come back a man.* You know. I didn't like that they only talked to the parents. I didn't like the way those other boys just stood off to the side like horses at auction. And I had been thinking of doing something anyway. Something else."

I stopped myself and held the cigarette upright while it unfurled smoke. It looked like the refinery towers that stood across the lake in the place I grew up.

"What?" she said. "What were you thinking about doing?"

"There was this place in Beaumont where my mom had worked before I was born. She'd talked about it a lot. A bar called Robicheaux's. She talked about her old boss there, Harper Robicheaux, what a great guy he was. He was this man-among-men type. She said she sang there sometimes. Then she'd sing for real. In the house."

"Did she sing good?"

"She did. I suppose she stopped when I came along."

"So, what did you do?"

"I left that recruitment office and took another bus over to Beaumont and found that place. Robicheaux's. It was really called Robicheaux's-on-the-Bayou. I went in and found that man she'd talked about, Harper, he owned it. I had to wait for him. He was like this powerful shady dude, but real friendly, with a lot of friends. I told him who my mother was, and he was nice about that. Asked me how she was, looked sad when I told him she'd passed. He asked me what I wanted and I said a job. I started off that way. I worked in his bar awhile, and when he decided I was smart he put me running playback."

She smoked and picked at her toenail. "Before you went to that bar, you were living with who?"

"Mr. and Mrs. Beidle. They ran the group home."

"Your mom was gone?"

"She'd died, years before. Got sick."

"Was it the same thing as you have?"

"I don't know. Maybe."

I put my cigarette out and followed the blood-colored line of salt rot staining the baseboards of the room. Mary-Anne hadn't gotten sick, or at any rate not like I was. When I was ten the people on the I-10 bridge said they reached out for her and she just nudged herself off the railing. She didn't make a sound, they said. One or two ran to the rail and saw her fall, her dress blossomed around her, five hundred feet down.

I've always imagined myself falling. That seems like a long way to fall without making a sound.

Rocky said, "What about your dad?"

"He was all right. He'd been a Marine. Korea. Died. Not in Korea. The refineries." I shrugged. "It was a long time ago."

I was in my twenties before I figured out that John Cady must have known I wasn't his. He was five-seven and I was six-three by my fifteenth birthday, and I didn't have his or Mary-

Anne's dark hair, or their chins, yet he never had me call him anything but Dad.

"This Robicheaux guy? You liked him, huh? I could see it just now. The way you talked about him."

"I guess I liked him all right. He was surprised as hell the first time he met me."

"Why?"

I rolled my eyes and sighed, but I wasn't minding it, telling these things I never told people. I started tugging off my boots. "Well," I grunted. "He was a big guy, like me, looked a lot like me, actually. Same face. He was surprised that we had the same face."

"He looked like you?"

"Just like me."

She thought on it a moment and I think missed my point. She said, "Weird. What was he like?"

"Smart. People liked him. Did good business with the Italians along the coast, up in New Orleans, and a lot of the bikers in Arkansas and Texas."

"Huh. What happened to him?"

"Somebody blew him up."

"Blew him up?"

"Just what I said."

"Sorry, Roy."

"That's all right."

"Sorry." She put out her cigarette and shoved her hands beneath her thighs, stretched out her legs, and the muscles in them pulled like ship cable.

I scratched my knee and felt my new face, the slack in the skin. She said, "I think I really kind of fucked things up."

"You don't need to see it that way," I said. I stood and walked to the sink, drank some water from it and washed my eyes—in the mirror my face was already beginning to look ordinary.

She peeked over her shoulder at me.

"You killed people before, Roy? Besides those men in that house."

I wiped my face and walked back. "A couple."

"How you feel about it?"

"Give me a break."

"Sorry." The disappointment in her glance was a little prodding. Death was making all my habits and consistencies unnecessary. Certain behaviors were changing. Like the way I was talking so much.

I said, "I feel like a soldier feels about it. People I did for, they weren't no innocent bystanders. They weren't anybody who hadn't put themselves in the place they were at. I look at it more like, they created a situation, and it required me to deal with it. They called it down."

She sniffled and breathed through her mouth, pinched her toes. "I been thinking that you're gonna leave us here."

I didn't reply to that. I stayed standing, though, so she might get the idea to go back to her room.

"You can tell me if you are, man. I mean, I get it. It makes sense. Even if you're sick. I mean, it don't make sense to hang around. I'm not mad or anything."

"You'll get a job. Take care of Tiffany. Win the lottery."

"I was looking at her earlier in there, and I kind of thought you were leaving us, and how bad a mess I'd made of everything. Even just following that dude Toby. He was queer. I thought it'd be all right. What a mess." She studied the smoldering cigarette. "But you know, man, it wasn't ever anything but a mess to begin with."

"I'm not leaving yet," I said.

"Well," she sighed. "It's not your mess, man. It's mine."

"You'll be all right."

"It never changed out there, you know? It was just always hot. Same fields, same grass. Nothing to do. I mean, I saw the rest of my life. Just day after day like that."

"I had a place like that," I said. But I winced, saying it, and I got angry with myself for talking along with her, angry mostly at the feeling that I wanted to talk about those empty fields and the flooding sun, about Loraine and Carmen. I wanted to say things about them but didn't know what.

She said, "Watching those kids out there today, on the beach? I kept thinking I just wanted a real life."

"It's all a real life."

"But you know what I mean. I want Tiffany to have that, too. Someplace regular."

"Then that's what'll happen."

Her face was dry now. She grinned and her eyes scrunched. "You look so weird with all your hair gone."

"I didn't recognize myself. That's good, I guess."

"You don't look so much like a psycho as before."

I turned up the A/C, and its churning rose louder and the glass in the window rattled. "You should get some sleep. We'll figure out something else tomorrow."

She held up a hand for me to help her rise, her eyes half-lidded and playful for a second, and that bothered me. She saw that it bothered me and stopped, walked real slow to the door. I couldn't help staring at her shorts, which had risen up her crack from sitting.

She paused and said, "If you want to leave, it's okay. It's all right. You did a lot for us, Roy. You can go ahead. We'll be fine."

I opened the door and said, "I might."

The man who'd been sitting on the stoop had moved to a grassy patch beside the sidewalk where he lay near a street lamp. Mosquitoes boiled in the tent of light beside him.

She turned back to me before going to her room, stopped herself from saying something.

I said, "If I'm here in the morning, it means I haven't left yet." I closed the door. After I was alone again a restlessness nagged me. I flipped through every television channel four or five times. I folded up all my clothes and put them in the dresser, one piece at a time, and then I took them all out and put them back in the duffel bag. I broke down and cleaned my .380 with a pencil and washrag. It felt like something was missing now, something hard to define, but noticeable by its absence.

I sensed that I had wronged myself by talking so much.

It looked like Emerald Shores kept a few regulars. The station wagon on the spare tires belonged to a family in number 2. The guy with the motorcycle kept aluminum foil across his windows, in number 8. Two older women shared number 12 and owned the late-model Chrysler on busted shocks whose front end sank forward like a drag racer. In the morning a guy across the way was prodding sausages on a short charcoal grill that burned greasy, peppered smoke everywhere. He sat on a folding chair and waved to me.

An old, gangly type who wore headbands and sandals, a tank top advertising Corona beer. The scent made me hungry and I walked over, saw he had a small stack of paper plates by his feet.

"This is kind of the breakfast the place offers, man. I'm Lance." He pulled out a plate and dropped two sausages on it.

"You work here?"

"Not really. I used to be married to Nancy in there. Woman who checked you in? She lets me stay here. She likes me to make breakfast for folks in the morning, though. They's no kitchen so I use the grill."

"All right. Thanks."

"She said you's with a couple little girls. They can get some too, they want."

I heard a door open and two children from number 2 stepped out with their father behind them. His hair jutted out and his face was flushed and swollen, his eyes bright red and shiny.

He looked me over, first thing.

He slapped the back of the boy's head. "Don't jump in front your sister. Let her get hers."

The kids were dazed and squinted in the light, as if they'd just been woken from a cave. Lance grinned at them and transferred two sausages onto a plate for first the girl, then the boy.

I'd just finished mine. The man said to the kids, "Get inside now."

"Mom said to get her some."

"She don't need no sausage. Tell her I said so." He took a plate from Lance and watched the kids walk back to their room. He had a big face, long and wide, a little skipping stone of a chin, and a fat, smooth neck that erased his jawline. His hair was longish and unkempt, a wifebeater T and stiff, smelly jeans stretched by a cannonball gut that made his back curve inward.

"Morning," said Lance.

"Yeah," the man said. "It is." He bit his sausage in half. Real hard-boiled, he wanted you to know. He had paranoid, naïve eyes. Used to be the biggest dog in a small yard, but his arms had gone soft now and were shaped like an old woman's thighs.

"Nothing on the *Kestrel*, I just found out," he said to me. "So that's a bust."

I looked at Lance and back to the other man. "I don't know what that is."

"It's an offshore rig. We came down here 'cause I was supposed to get on one for Cities Service. But I get here and they say they never hired me. I said I got a letter. They tell me the letter doesn't say what it says." He looked to Lance for vindication. "And I'm *holding* it." He finished his sausages and set the paper plate down on the parking lot.

He saw me reaching for my cigarettes. "Got an extra?"

I gave him one.

"Where you from? I figured you must work a rig."

"Nah. I'm on vacation."

"Where from?"

"Louisiana."

"What part?"

"New Orleans."

"I'm sorry for you, man. Been there before. All that rain and the Catholics and niggers."

"It can swallow up some folks," I said. "You have to know what's what."

"I knew a boy from New Orleans. Shot himself in the *thigh*. That boy was a *fool*."

"Must be why they made him leave."

His brow crinkled as he tried to suss out my meaning. I realized that another guy had come out, the one with the motorcycle, number 8, where the aluminum foil flattened against the window glass. He was young and scrawny, long-haired, and he stayed back a little, watching us in big sunglasses. The other man was still eyeing me, trying to understand what exactly I had said to insult him.

"How many kids you got in that hotel room?" I asked, kind of mockingly.

"Just the two. And a woman." He shook his head. "Gets fatter every day." As a gesture of concession, he started talking about his wife. He'd had to make a point to her about swimwear a few days back, and she hadn't left the room since. "She wants to act like I hurt her feelings or something. You know how they get."

I flicked away my cigarette and walked back to my room. The boy from number 8 had bent down to ask Lance a question, and the other man just stood there looking around, turning back and forth, bewildered that no one was listening to him talk about his wife.

Closing my door, I saw that the long-haired kid was watching me now, and I looked back at him.

He grinned like we were old friends. He shot me with a finger gun.

When the girls woke up they ate and got dressed and we didn't really know what to do with ourselves. I figured the kid should get to see the beach. So I threw on torn jeans and wore them with a bright Hawaiian-style shirt I'd bought with a pair of sandals the day before, and I went down to the beach with them. There was no good reason for me to do this, but I still had the time to kill, and also an urge to see what the little girl made of the ocean and the sand. I was curious.

The father from number 2 was standing outside his room with a Michelob and he nodded to me on our way out. "Nice shirt," he said, flipping his chin up.

We walked five blocks and crossed a median to the pocket beach off the road. Loose newspaper and food wrappers caught by the sandspurs shook in the breeze, and hairy sheaths of love grass fenced the sandy decline toward the ocean. Tiffany smiled, skipped beside Rocky, and pointed. The ocean sloshing up and reaching back forever.

Rocky took off her shorts and shirt, and she saw me watching and I glanced away. Her bikini was pretty skimpy, four triangles of red fabric, and my breath went deep at the sight. Deceptive curves and slim lines drew her, dancer's muscles gone red across her pale skin where the sun warmed it, her cheeks and nose flushed, and the sun off her hair struck gold and white reflections. She squatted and folded her clothes on the ground with a propriety that struck me as massively erotic. She had broad shoulders for her size and her back was a hilly tract of muscle, the kind you have to earn.

I sat back in a shallow sandbed. I'd brought two cans of Coors and popped one while Tiffany ran out to the tide, totally astonished and almost tripping over her own feet. Rocky took her out to the water and they'd be chased back up by the dying waves, the girl's laughter flung like bells, a sound of pure thrill that didn't seem foolish.

When Rocky got splashed her suit clung to her like wet tissue and I could make out her nipples and the crease of her ass. She waved to me, stood there with her sister while the waves flopped over them, coating them with sparklers, the girl shriek-laughing, and the blue and purple waters behind them were scored with foam and drew out so totally that you could imagine a time the entire planet was only sea and sky. But a boat towing a skier crossed the horizon, and through the mists to the east you could make out an offshore rig.

They came back up the shore. Rocky sat with Tiffany to try showing her how to build sand castles. Tiffany pointed out at the Gulf and said, "Where's it go?"

"Into the ocean."

"What's that?"

"More water."

"Where's *it* go?"

"Oh, hush," said Rocky, and she tickled the girl's ribs.

Rocky's legs were stretched out while she packed the wet sand, and it was hard not to look at her so I found things on the beach. A patch of broom sage where something glittered. A pair of fat little boys scuttling into the surf. Gulls riding thermals, swooping to skim the surface with their bills. A rainbow-colored kite held by someone far down the beach, someone I couldn't see. The kite wobbled and danced and looped in tight circles, and Tiffany saw it and poked up at it with her finger.

A pack of boys walked by, flipping a football, and they all quieted and stared at Rocky as they passed. She noticed them and started showing Tiffany how to pack the sand.

I took off my shirt and lay prone to the light. Tried to imagine my cells storing up the sunshine.

Rocky said, "What're those scars from?"

"Which ones?"

"Them round ones up your side."

I fingered the dimpled skin and kept my eyes closed to the sun. "Buckshot."

"Like a shotgun?"

"It was far off. They just peppered me."

"What about that other? On your shoulder."

"Knife."

"That must have been a big knife."

"It was."

"And that one up on your leg?"

"Dog."

"I knew it. I figured that one was a dog. Did you kill it?"

"The dog?"

"Yeah."

"I don't remember." But I did.

I waited for her to ask me something else, and when she didn't say anything I peeked through my lids and saw she'd gone back to focusing on Tiffany.

After my beers were gone I dozed in and out for a few minutes, and when I woke Rocky was on her back, sunning herself beside me. Little beads of water and sand clung to her skin, and sweat had gathered in a pool at her navel. I had to get away from that, and I walked out to the water.

Tiffany cheered and ran beside me, hopping. The rainbow kite was still up there, jabbing and slicing the pale gold air.

The girl stopped at the break and reached up her arms, groaned as if by effort she could reach my shoulders. Then I held her above the water, acting like I'd toss her out into the ocean, and she screamed and laughed at once. I felt like yelling something with her, but I didn't. I pinched her nose and threw us both into the waves, holding her up while I went under and the briny water poured over me, and she laughed and spat and gasped with amazement, unsure, then asked for it again.

For the rest of the day, her weight echoed in my empty hands, light but dense, her throes and kicks. I walked her back up the beach, and once in a while the little girl would commit a gesture that seemed very womanly, like pulling wet hair behind her ear or straightening her swimsuit with a brief, serious face.

Rocky lay out on the sandbed, shining at us.

I remember a buddy of mine once telling me that every woman you loved was a mother and sister you didn't have, at once, and that what you were always really looking for was the female part of yourself, your female animal or something. This guy could get away with saying something like that because he was a junkie and read books.

When we walked home it was impossible to avoid falling back and watching Rocky from behind in that swimsuit, but I don't think I could have actually touched her.

In late afternoon we ate fried shrimp and oyster po'boys, and I took them to the arcade along the piers. They played Whac-a-Mole and Ms. Pac-Man, tossed rings. I wandered the pier but didn't let them out of my sight.

Some black men perched along the pier with fishing poles, and an overturned rowboat sat on the beach below. There was a hole in it and I could hear a cat mewling through the hole, and thousands of scarlet prize tickets were scattered on the sands.

Later at night, we watched a movie with I think Richard Boone on the television, and by the time I left them they were tired and pleased-looking, and I realized I felt good about that.

Back in my room I felt good about the way I'd left them.

Then I was dogged by something I couldn't put into words. Like I'd forgotten something important, but didn't know what.

I walked outside and looked through the spotted night, the hot wind stirring the palms and coursing out to the heavenriver of stars. I walked.

Antique grain elevators and warehouses stood around the South from the old days of cotton-exporting, and some of the elevators had floodlights. Salt rain and the smells of shrimp and oyster hauls hung in the air. A man was helping his friend walk with an arm around his shoulder.

The clunk of my boots on asphalt sounded like a clock's hand. A smoke-gray cat kept pace with me on the opposite sidewalk for a while. On a bus bench an old bearded guy was drinking from a paper bag and weeping. He told me he was happy. He'd gotten out of prison that day.

When I got back to my room it was so quiet the alarm clock's tick seemed to reverberate, and the small sound said to me that it was late, later, then later still.

Time had passed. I was old.

In the morning I was up before the girls and I watched dawn break on the bay, where the water yellowed a little, and the shrimping fleets spread out into it, small schooners with bony jibs and baggy nets. These ships crawled out into the sea with the slow and coordinated process of a natural migration. The sun in the evening or the sun in the morning charged the sky with hysterical colors, green and purple and hot reds and oranges, unreal, the clouds of the old MGM Westerns.

Slow movements. Changing colors.

I was noticing new things.

Rocky said that she guessed she should start looking for a job today, but I told her we should all go to the beach instead, and we did.

That evening we met two more regulars, old women who shared the Chrysler with the broken antenna. Their names were Dehra and Nonie Elliot, sisters with the same wiry gray hair in the same cauliflower-shaped style, and they dressed in stiff dark fabrics like clergy, wore thick crucifixes around their necks.

Lance had been grilling some burgers and I'd brought a six-pack of Coors outside. The girls came, too, and after watching Tiffany from the window of room 12, the two sisters ventured out to meet her.

They bent at their waists to shake hands with Tiffany, who bit her thumb kind of demurely.

They had gentle, amused faces, carried hunched backs with the dignity of quiet burdens. The one named Dehra wore glasses and tended to speak out more.

You look less suspicious when you're willing to meet people.

Dehra told me, "We have four sisters who're nuns at the Sisters of St. Joseph in Houston. We used to live in Denton but we sold our parents' house. We thought we'd buy a place in Florida, but you know, we've just been driving around Texas, really."

"Well, we wanted to be close to our sisters," Nonie said.

"That's true. But we've been here three weeks."

"We keep meaning to get a more permanent place."

"I don't know why. But we can't seem to get up the energy to find one."

There was something girlish about them, a lack of guile in their calm, sexless faces. "Do you go to the beach much?" I asked.

"Oh, my no. We don't really care for the sun."

She said that as her sister tried to offer Tiffany some clove gum while the girl moved shyly around Rocky's legs. I had the fleeting urge to tell this woman about my lungs.

Lance had set up a folding card table and Nancy brought out a sack of hamburger buns, ketchup and mustard, paper plates. She set them on the table and looked me over.

"I remember just the other day you had all that hair. Look at you. You afraid somebody's going to recognize you?"

I said, "Too hot around here for all that hair."

Lance flipped the burgers and said, "I bet these'll be as good as the place in Austin. Greenbelt Grill. You 'member that, baby?"

Nancy flexed her eyebrows at him and frowned.

He looked at me and said, "It's this country-cookin' place we used to go to." He turned back to Nancy and said, "You 'member?"

She just sighed real loud and rolled her eyes at him in a pitying way, as if he'd embarrassed himself. She walked back to the office.

Tiffany was laughing with the old sisters now, and she was making them laugh.

"She used to be a lot different," Lance said. "She straightened up before me and I guess she's taken it a little far, maybe. I know what you're thinking, but I don't see Nancy just like she is now, you understand. I see all the Nancy I ever knew, and there were all sorts of her. She likes that I got all that history, even if she acts like she don't."

Rocky had come outside, and so had the kid from room 8. He had long red hair and kind of a bookish quality, delicate, and the torn jeans and biker boots he wore seemed severely out of place.

They started talking to each other against the wall by the rooms, and he said something and Rocky laughed. The boy wore a long-sleeved gray T-shirt and his narrow shoulders hunched a little, hands in pockets.

He saw me looking and waved. Rocky seemed nervous.

The father from room 2 came out. He shut the door behind him, only opening it enough to slip out. His tongue moved over his lips as he surveyed the grub.

He stood by the grill and sort of looked around at everybody. "We all begging hamburgers like starving dogs!" he announced to nobody in particular, kept an eye out for some reaction, and when there was none he tried to look occupied in thought.

"I'm Tray," the boy with the red hair said to me. He held out a hand, and his eyes blinked from thin gray pockets. Rocky picked up one of my beers and sipped it.

I shook the boy's hand. "Tray Jones," he said, and his eyes darted over my forearms, back to my stare, and he seemed like he wanted to tell me something. He was so thin I had the impression his shirt weighed him down. He said, "Most people call me Killer."

"Of course they do," I said.

The father took the next three hamburgers. I thought about saying something, but when I saw he was taking them back to the room I was glad he was leaving and let it pass.

He had them piled on a single plate and he glanced over his shoulder to us as he walked to his room and unlocked it, peeking back to me again when he slipped inside, just opening the door a few inches and sliding through.

Tray Jones was still standing beside me. "You seen ole boy's kids in there? Look like they ain't eat right in a while."

I nodded. Rocky sat on the stoop watching the old ladies talk to Tiffany.

He took out a pack of menthols and offered me one. I turned it down. He lit it and said, "Where'd you do your time, brah?"

"What?"

"It's cool, man. I can always tell a natural convict. Way you ate your sausages, man." He chuckled. "You know?"

I took a cigarette. "Nowhere."

"Oh, yeah. Okay." He nodded, offered me a light. His nails were bit to the quick, his shirt pulled down past thin wrists. I figured he'd have tracks up those arms. "I went down in Rowan, Oklahoma," he said. "Do yourself a favor and stick to the south."

"How old are you?"

"Twenty-six last March."

"What were you doing in Rowan?"

"Oh." He raised his shoulders to hit the cigarette. "Doing some work this ole boy I used to run with. My partner. We were doing good till he gets in a fight this bar. They come to take him, want to look in his car. I didn't even know how it started. I's sleeping in the backseat."

"Huh."

Lance said, "We got three more ready."

I told the girls to go ahead and eat. The old women walked Tiffany up to the table and helped her fix a burger. Tray still stood beside me.

I was wondering what this kid wanted from me.

"I got some people here now," he said. "I got some people I know here."

I didn't say anything and finished my beer.

"You know you remind me of, man?" he said.

I raised my eyebrow and twisted off a fresh cap.

"Guy from the movies. What's that guy? He was in the movie about the cockfighter. And the other. Ole boy driving around with a head in the car."

I thought for a second. "That guy looks like a horse."

"But not in a bad way, really."

"Here." I handed him a beer and took the rest off to my room. I wasn't hungry.

The sky was a bottomless red and shadows revolved on the cracked asphalt.

After midnight I'd cracked a fresh bottle of Jameson because I didn't sleep anymore unless I had a load on. I was well into the bottle's second half and time began to pool and flood for me, lost moments, fantasies that opened and closed like puzzle boxes, so I have trouble remembering the exact procession of events. There was a mania to my thoughts, though. I felt like crying but couldn't quite make it happen. When I first saw the X-rays I had walked out the doctor's office in a hurry, pushed through the door as soon as I heard the words *small-cell lung carcinomas*.

Now I wanted to know how much time I had. I must have called information for the doctor's home number.

I have some recollection of being fired up and cursing, and that a man on the phone sounded like he was asleep, and I could hear a woman's voice behind him. I think I had to remind him who I was, and who had referred me to him.

I believe I said something like, "How long? How long do I have?"

He said he didn't know and couldn't say and tried to explain to me the necessity of further tests, biopsies. Yes, the overwhelming odds were that I had small-cell carcinomas. I think he tried to convince me to come back in.

"You just ran out the office, last time. We didn't get a chance to really get into the treatment options."

I think I remember being deeply insulted by his inability to answer me, feeling he was patronizing me, and all of a sudden I had great hatred for this man. I admit that certain essential connections weren't firing in my head at the time. But I pictured the pink, freshly scrubbed look of him, the gray hair trimmed and neatly parted, the cold, practiced way he'd told me about my death.

It just seemed like for a second, in that dark, salt-ridden motel room, in the middle of the night, with my breath hot against the telephone, I had located the main villain, the enemy of my whole life.

And I think, now, that I just wanted to hear him be scared. Like me.

"*You fucking sawbones quack motherfucker,*" I said. "You want me to come back in? I'll come back in. Then we'll see about getting a straight answer."

He protested my anger, argued his innocence.

"I got the address right here, you prick. 2341 Royale. Probably a big house. Of course it is."

"*What?* No, no—listen—"

"Your old lady know about the gambling? She know how deep you're in for? You degenerate prick."

"Now. Now, listen—just stop a minute—"

I think that's around when I slammed the phone down. I must have flung it across the room, because the next morning it was in pieces against the far wall, the line ripped from its socket.

When I woke the next day the sun was rising and the room was hot, my pillow soaked in sweat. I was shirtless and my chest had red abrasions all over it, scratches, as if something wild had been at me. I looked at my fingernails and the marks on my chest. The bottle lay on the floor, and I dimly questioned the displacement of the telephone.

I experienced the murky horror that comes with certain hangovers, where you wonder what exactly you've been up to, what tickets you've written.

But I didn't remember making any calls. I chalked the phone up to the ordinary collateral damage that occurs around delicate objects when you drink like that.

bought newspapers. A local one for the classifieds, the *Houston Chronicle*, and *The Times-Picayune* out of New Orleans.

The Times-Picayune had a brief story saying that Sienkiewicz was wanted for questioning in an ongoing probe.

The implication was that he'd skipped town.

No mention of Stan Ptitko. Nothing about Angelo or the other men or the woman and what happened at Sienkiewicz's house in Jefferson Heights.

I pondered what Stan was doing. If he had people out looking for us. How many would that be, and how far could they search. It didn't matter, all told; we were a needle in a haystack.

I still had that folder I took from Sienkiewicz's house, but I didn't see any real play in it. Maybe I'd mail it to the D.A. before heading down Mexico way.

I kept telling myself I'd leave them. First, it was when I'd gotten them a place to stay for a while. Then I decided it would be once Rocky got a job.

I spread the classifieds on the bed.

"Here's one for a hostess. There's another. Babysitter. You could do that."

She paced back and forth in front of the window. Wearing those little shorts again. Nancy had found a few old board games in the office, and Nonie and Dehra asked if they could have Tiffany for a few hours.

"What?" I said.

"I mean, what do I do?" she said.

"You dress nice and you go in and ask for an application. You bring a pen and fill it out."

"But, I mean. What do I fill out? I ain't had a job before, Roy."

I had to think on this.

I took a yellow pad from the nightstand drawer and tapped the pencil on my teeth. I wrote down the names of two places. One was a bar in Morgan City, and the other was a barbeque joint in New Orleans. Both of them had burned to the ground over the last few years. I'd watched, matter of fact.

I handed it off to her. "That's where you worked. Make a timeline for yourself. You just tell them the places are closed now. And you stayed at each till they closed, 'cause that's the type of worker you are—a sticker. You're loyal."

She sat on the bed and she shook her head as if arguing it.

"I don't know, though, Roy—I just don't know what to do. I *don't know how* to do this."

"Well, you're going to have to teach yourself."

Her eyes had teared up and took a ninety-yard stare. I thought about everything I didn't know about her, and what parts of her had led her to Sienkiewicz's house. At the least it was real poor judgment, but it could be something worse.

"All you do is act like a charmer when they talk to you. You know how to do that."

Her eyes flickered over to me and they looked wild, rapt with simmering hysteria. I thought of how quick her laugh could become desperate.

"You got to think of it this way. The dumbest sons of bitches on earth can get jobs. You just got to get out there and do it."

She nodded and wiped her eyes, stared at the curtains.

We heard sirens whisk by the window, and the bed squeaked as I got up.

"You could stay in here awhile," she said. "Them ladies are going to watch Tiffany."

I paused at the door and she stretched her legs, sat back on her elbows, and the bed squeaked again. I gave her a look of warning about whatever she was doing with her legs.

Then she started talking. "I never saw my dad. My mom told me a couple different stories about him. In one he was in prison, and in the other he was dead. My mom met Gary at the club she's working. I used to sit in the backseat sometimes. When she'd be out with somebody. Drove around in backseats. Every time I want to say Gary was evil, I always think about him being lazy. This big, fat, lazy fucker. Got fatter every year. Started breathing hard if he had to look for the remote. I think types of laziness is evil."

I moved back from the door, let myself sit down, and offered her another Camel. She waited till she'd taken the first hit and scraped her tongue along her teeth.

"My mom went away about four years ago. I mean, Gary talked like she ran off. Maybe she did. She might of went out one night and not come back. I think something happened to her."

We ashed at the same time and the tip of her cigarette was shuddering.

"What he did once. He decided he was gonna raise rabbits. He's living on something from the state. He did something at the plants once but hurt his leg, so he's living off that mostly. My mom thought it was a stupid idea. She worked at a club in Beaumont. There were nights I know where she didn't come home. So maybe she did run off. Maybe she was thinking about those rabbits."

She crossed her legs and I turned my eyes to the curtains.

"He spent some money. Made me get out there and help him build these fences with chicken wire, mow down all the area behind the house with a push mower he had to borrow. All that sun. We spent a few weeks building like a chicken coop for them all, and what he said was that you got a few of these big special kind of rabbit, and you put them in there, maybe just two, and in a couple months you had a whole bunch of rabbits. You just fed them and watered them. Sold them in town. Meat and fur, 'cause these kinds of rabbits had good fur. Me and mom were both shocked when that was pretty much what happened. I was eleven then, I guess. We didn't have no dogs or cats and I liked having all those bunnies around. They were huge. If you held them under their arms and let them hang with their toes touching the ground, they'd come up to your shoulders. White and black and spotted rabbits. He'd keep making up numbers and writing them on paper at the kitchen table, trying to think up how much his first litter would be worth, spending it already. But this was all before August, when the heat gets so bad, and the grass drying out and the yard turning to dirt. There were too many of them to feed, so he took half out. He had Mom and me go with him into Lake Charles to sell this batch, a bunch of wire cages in his truck. He doesn't get as much as he figures. Not nearly. The stores that sell fur coats tell him it doesn't work like that. They all go to the butcher, cheap. So he's upset and Mom's upset that he didn't get near as much as he thought. I remember feeling so bad for those things when we were at the meat place and the skinned animals hung everywhere. Him and Mom are so pissed and he says, 'Fuck it. Let's go get a drink.' And they go to do that, and I stay in the room. That's what I was thinking about just now, next door in there. I was thinking about sitting alone in that room. Because I was there a couple days. I just stayed in there watching TV and I'd eat cereal at the breakfast counter in the mornings. I hate waiting for things. They come back two days later and they look like hell, pissed off, their clothes are wrecked. Stink. So now whatever money he did get was gone and she needed to get back to work, and we all went back to Orange.

"I was thinking about that. Sitting in that room. Like sitting in the backseat of a car." She picked at a fingernail and fiddled with her cigarette.

"But, Gary's rabbits—when we got back first thing we see is the backyard is full of birds. A bunch of birds in there, a couple big vultures that made me start crying just to look at. He hollered at them and got them off and I saw one of the vultures tug a strip of meat off as it flapped away. All the rabbits were splayed out in the backyard. They were all stretched out on the ground, more than a dozen, just lying there. They were all chewed up. Come to find out they'd overheated, didn't have water, just like suffocated. I remember my mom swatting him with her purse. She was crying, she was so mad. I'd been crying since we drove up and saw the big birds, but then I think I was screaming. We were both screaming at him and crying, and he just looked pathetic, all fat and hungover and teary. Anyway, that's what he was like. I think that was the last time he tried to make any money. Besides selling shitty weed he grew behind the house."

She flipped some bangs off her forehead, and she looked up. The downturn of her lips was coarse, a little clumsy, and the heavy way her lids sat on her eyes spoke to very specific things.

I stood and went to the door. Parts of me wished that I wanted her, and whatever held me back was hard to put into words. I didn't want to think about it.

"Get some sleep," I said.

Back in my room I realized that if her mother had left four years ago, it would have been before Tiffany was born. I didn't want to think about that, either.

I shot up in bed, breath trapped. Police lights flashed outside the curtains, red and blue strobing the room. The lights were silent but I was deafened by the pulse booming through my ears.

I rolled off the bed and dug out the lockbox and grabbed my .380, chambered a round. I squatted next to the metal door, both hands on the gun, and focused on quelling my breathing, getting a deep, slow rhythm going. You line the front sight with the back sight by making two parallel bars of light frame the front. Exhale and squeeze the trigger, like making a fist. Don't pull.

I waited for the knock. Far voices came from outside, low, official, and I crawled to the window, peeked through the edges.

Two police cruisers parked in front of room 2. Another sat on the street, blocking the driveway, all of them creating a paranoid carnival with their lights.

There was an ambulance, too.

Nancy stood outside in a long robe, her arms folded. Lance put a hand on her shoulder, and they watched from the purple shadows around his room. Down the way, the door to room 2 was open. This was where the commotion centered.

By and by two deputies escorted the father out. His eye was blackened and he was shirtless, his hands cuffed in back, big gut spilling over his jeans. He looked dismayed, humble and frightened.

Directly after him two paramedics wheeled a gurney out the room, a thing on it covered by a sheet. One of her arms hung out from under the sheet, and her hand was like a tiny claw on the end of that massive hock. The skin flashed blue and red in the night.

I spotted the kids watching things from the backseat of a cruiser, where the mesh gate between seats crosshatched their faces in shadow. I closed the curtain and stepped away from the window.

I couldn't sleep and flipped stations on the television for the better part of an hour, but I couldn't follow anything on the screen. The cop lights were gone. I stepped out to check if Nancy or Lance was still around, to see if I could find out what had happened in number 2.

The only person outside was the red-haired boy, Killer Tray, standing beside his door smoking a cigarette and pulling on a bottle of Lone Star. He lifted the beer and wiggled it, cocked his head.

I wasn't going to sleep, I could tell, and the prospect of a cold brew drew me across the lot.

He said, "She was like that awhile," nodding down the way to number 2, where yellow police tape crossed over the door. He stepped inside for a second and came back with a fresh beer, handed it off to me.

"What'd he do?" I asked him. The beer was not quite cold enough but soothing just the same.

He shrugged. "It took awhile. One of the kids finally said something to Nancy." He hit his cigarette with a laconic sort of attitude, a reserve he'd rehearsed but not yet mastered. "Cops took the kids. Took him, too. They told Nancy there were bruises around her midsection."

What I remembered about the man then was how helpless he'd seemed, and how you could tell that helplessness had made him cruel.

"Those girls are your nieces?" The kid's voice was high with an extravagant drawl, a practiced Texan.

"Yeah."

"You just out for vacation, huh? I's talking to your oldest one. She said you brought them out for the beach. Said her daddy died."

I nodded. A warm breeze rustled the police tape across the door, palm leaves rattled.

"Sorry to hear it." He flipped his butt across the lot and ran fingers through his hair. "I been on vacation, too. Laying low."

I let that go, took a drink of the Lone Star.

"What were you sent up for, you don't mind my asking?"

I flicked him a hard stare, rolled my eyes at the question.

"Yeah. No sweat, brah." He scratched at his neck and the skin was grated, shaded to ash tones and given a grainy quality in the pale buzzing light. He hadn't been to the beach much. The long red hair was feminine on his slight frame and his features were all about deprivation, angles of want. But maybe that beggary tugged some sympathy from me, because I remembered how hard I worked not to seem scared at his age.

"Reason I ask," he said, "I's wondering if you're looking for work at all. Like if you want to earn. While you're, you know, on vacation."

I looked at him out the side of my vision, the kid wispy, gray. He cocked an eyebrow with a bit of moxie that showed me something. Mostly I just wanted another beer.

"What you got, Killer?"

In his aluminum-shuttered room, a garbage bag spilled some clothes and a drawstring laundry bag looked filled with sharp, heavy objects. Bungee cord laced the sack for strapping to his bike. Not much else in the room but two books and some sketchings on the table. *Modern Electronic Alarms,* read the cover of one. The other was white and titled *777 and other Kabbalistic Writings.* Pages of yellow legal paper bore drawings, ink scribbles and diagrams, odd doodles.

"Man, I knew you was down. I could just tell. I got that eye for it."

I'd taken another of his beers and lit a cigarette, watched as he shuffled together his papers and stacked them on the books. He had a kind of fastidious, finicky way with his hands, making the papers stack even on all sides, having to square off the angles of the books to the surface of the table. He almost seemed bashful about that, like he couldn't help himself. His round, wire-frame glasses added to this schoolboy air, the kind of intellectual particular to a junk habit.

"All right. Here it is, man. Mr. Robicheaux. The thing.

What do you think I do, man? I mean, how you think I make do?"

I just hit the cigarette and let smoke unroll over my face while I stared at him. "I can't imagine."

"All right. This right here, man. This is what I do. I am a thief, and a real, real fucking good one."

I didn't offer a response except to squint into the smoke drifting between us.

"Okay, okay. You're saying, 'So what?' I know. You're saying, 'Good for you.' Well, my trip is that I'm not going to spend any part of my life in a cage again. My thing is that I don't make a run at something unless it's *bona fide,* unless there's no risk and large reward." He pulled out some yellow legal sheets with drawings of room layouts, crude maps. A lot of good thieves were junkies. When they were on top of their habits, they could be effective professionals, but it never lasted. They'd stay functionally clean, pull a few jobs, and at some point get too successful, overdo the junk and get busted, start the cycle over when they got out. I noticed the webs between Tray's fingers had a few little welts on them, like chigger bites. "I had this partner, man. Good guy. Solid. He was kind of like, well, he would have been what you'd call the muscle of the operation, more or less. He brought me up. Did transpo, bankrolled scores sometimes. A jobber. Real good guy."

Behind him the foil on the windows held dull, pleated reflections of us, and I almost asked him why he kept it there.

"He's gone now, but we were a good team. He's over. Some ole boys dumped him in a swamp in Alabama." I'd taken him for a half-ass grifter, but at the mention of his buddy gloom wafted over his eyes and I thought the kid was lonely, and that reminded me of my old self, too. He hadn't quite learned how to carry it yet. He pretended to relinquish things he really hadn't. He said, "Only now I got some things going. I got prospects."

"What do you steal?" I said.

He twitched his face like the question was absurd. "Pharmaceuticals, man."

"You take down doctors."

He shrugged, held the expression to emphasize its obviousness. "Listen, man. The thing is, swear to God, I can turn raw product around in two, three days. Tops. I mean like thirty thousand dollars, man. I mean like there's this guy runs a clinic on Broadway. I know a cleaning lady there, man."

I didn't say anything, and he took that as encouragement.

"In Corpus and Houston, I can move it. Three days. Thirty might be a low estimate, really. This guy—he's like the doctor for every legit dude owns a vacation spot here. Their broads, them housewives. He's the guy that gets them their drugs. Keeps a sampler dope pharmacy stocked on the premises. I'm talking now benzies, dexies, biphetamine. Amphetamine. Ecstasy. You know what that is? I got this place airtight, man. My maid, she fronts me the info on their alarm system. I got Polaroids. It's nothing, man. Contact alarm. I do those in my sleep. Nothing to it."

"What do you need me for?"

"Okay. All right." He put out his smoke and lit another, shuffled some papers on the desk and showed me a crude schematic, a room plan. "I need somebody to front a van, and I need a fixer. Somebody to help me get in, open the door from the outside once I'm in. Help me move it. My thing is I hide in the place till they lock up and close. I come out, bypass the alarm—you just make a closed circuit. Moving the stuff—we got to do it fast. From the back door to the van. And really, what a guy like you would really help with is *moving* the stuff. I got all the clients, but, you know, the people interested in this stuff are more or less scum-of-the-earth. Not to be trusted. You know? Wilson was great for all that. A big dude, like you. Always strapped. Nobody would try ripping off Wilson. Everybody thinks they'll rip me, though. So. You know. I think it's just that this type of thing goes a lot smoother if there's a big killermanjaro across the table when the deal goes down. A guy like you."

"What makes you think you could trust me?"

"I knew you was a convict. But I seen you with your nieces, man. Way you are with them girls. You're a definite white man. You want to make some bank for your people, I figure. You got that sense about you, but also kind of hard. You ain't no junkie. I could tell that."

I tapped my fingers on the table. A hot wind cooed outside.

"How'd you come to do this, Tray?"

He laughed to himself. Tiny teeth almost appeared to flutter.

"I's in a group home in Houston. Ran off when I's fifteen. Started boosting. Did all right for a while. Just crashed wherever. Had some other kids I knew. One day I meet Wilson. I'm seventeen. Figure I won't see twenty. I'm in this Maison Blanche, right, boosting a couple watches. I look back on it and I was real obvious, but back then I'm thinking I'm smooth. Anyway, I'm loaded down with a couple hundred bucks' worth, this big dude passes by me, just behind me, and he like jabs me in the back and says, 'Nix, kid.' He keeps walking. Freaks me out. So I unload the stuff, empty it out in the clothes racks, and when I'm walking out, sure enough, two security guys stop me, check me out. But I'm clean. I get out the store and the big guy's out there. He had this cool El Dorado he's standing by, smoking. He was watching me the whole time. Said the store security was, too. So that's Wilson, right? And he's like the professional. And I'm like the amateur. Rolled with him almost eight years. Good times. Taught me a lot."

He pulled two more beers out for us.

"But, like I said. They got Willie-Son in Alabama." He shook his head and upended the beer. I could see it clearly, the orphan in him. The deprivation.

I set down my bottle and leaned forward. "Look, kid. You seem like a good clipper to me. But you got the wrong idea. I threw off all that illegality a while back."

"Oh, come on, man."

"It's true. I got to take care of them girls now, and we're just down for some sun and waves. Then we're moving on. I got no use for what you're talking about."

Dismay snuffed the light in his eyes, hung his mouth open a bit. "You're kidding me."

I shook my head, stood and finished the beer, set the bottle on the table beside his books. "I wish you all the luck with it, though. Keep your head on a swivel."

I'd turned to the door and he said, "You could take care of them girls a lot better with this score. You don't need fifteen grand, man?"

I looked over my shoulder and said, "Not where I'm going." I thanked him for the beer and left the room.

The wind through the trees was a sparse sound and behind it sat a great silence, and the small sounds were like trinkets scattered across that silence. I looked along the walls at all the red metal doors under the humming light, and the yellow tape across number 2, a couple of cars, the kid's motorcycle. The open air felt confining.

Acouple days later a newspaper convinced me to finally ditch the girls. Rocky had gone on the job hunt downtown. Third day in a row. I'd seen her off on the bus because I wanted her to get used to making her own way around town. Nancy had gone to the grocery store and rented a couple cartoon movies for Tiffany. She came to the girls' room and asked if Tiffany wanted to watch *Cinderella* on the VCR in her office. The two old sisters were waiting there, and I watched Tiffany skip behind as they crossed to the parking lot. They'd been spending a lot of time with her. The little one seemed to light up around those older women and they sure delighted in her presence.

I was sitting out in the parking lot, getting sun—I'd gotten in the habit of soaking my chest in sunshine, as if it could burn my insides clean. I sipped JW in a paper cup, perusing the *Houston Chronicle* and *Times-Picayune*. No news about the fed's investigation into the ports. Nothing about Stan Ptitko or the house in Jefferson Heights.

I'd started drinking more JW than usual. I didn't even wait for noon anymore. One pull on the bottle would jump-start the morning. I found it necessary to rouse my spirit that way. And it helped me sit still while I took the sun.

At the end of the *Chronicle*'s crime report, shoved into the bottom right:

Reclusive Man Found Shot in Home;
Wife, Daughters Missing

The body of Gary Benoit, of Orange, Texas, was found in his home off Big Lake Road on Thursday by two local boys. Coroner states that Mr. Benoit had been shot once in the stomach, and an animal had apparently come upon the scene first. Deputies confirmed that it had taken several days to come across the body because the deceased had no neighbors or employment. The sheriff's office has released no other information, but Mr. Benoit's wife, Charmane, is wanted for questioning, and they are seeking any information as to the whereabouts of his infant daughter, Tiffany, and stepdaughter Raquel, 18.

My heart plopped into my stomach like a stone. Rocky's tears took on a whole new context. I recalled the distances in her face when she'd sat in my room and talked about her life, the shock and stuttering and wide, flitting eyes. Some people's crazy was worse than others.

This is why you make rules, why you stay mobile and ready to walk. I crushed the papers and tossed them into the oil-drum trash can standing in an alcove between rooms. Whatever shred of sense I still had screamed for me to light out, ditch this situation.

That's what I did.

I threw my things in the duffel bag, took the lockbox and my JW. Scoped out the motel from my window and when the coast was clear tossed my things in the truck and pulled out the lot, made sure that I didn't look in my rearview mirror until Emerald Shores was out of sight.

My pulse thrummed like I was making a jailbreak, and alongside that this incoherent disappointment curdled my gut. There'd been something with her that had set off my imagination, I admitted, some kind of dumb hope in a bad place. A cure.

That was over.

It didn't matter, I told myself. Now it was just me and Texas. Me and cancer.

Several blocks away I pulled into an alley and wiped down the gun and silencer she'd taken, smashed it, and threw the pieces in different Dumpsters.

When I reached the highway I drove north on 45 and pretended I didn't know why.

B y the town of Teague I was considerably buzzed and my thought-to-action ratio had sped up so that I was making the phone call before I could stop myself. I hadn't been to Dallas in years, but some time ago I'd paid an investigator I knew to find out where she was. I'd kept the information in my lockbox. I don't know why I did that, really. When I hit Dallas I checked a phone book and confirmed the address. Her husband's name. Everybody had listings in those days.

"I was just passing through here, really. Thought I'd call . . . Ran into somebody. Clyde in Beaumont. He just said you lived here. Got married—that's great. I was just passing through. You're in the phone book— Yeah. *Surprise* . . . I don't do that anymore—I weld, mostly. In a couple unions. I's down in Galveston, on a rig. Coming back up through. Remembered you were here. Had the time to kill— Listen, how'd you feel about getting some lunch? No, no— Just to say hi . . . No. I don't do that anymore."

*   *   *

A neighborhood in the Brentwood area, oilmen and minor celebrities, CEOs, semiretired politicians, wives playing tennis. A former heavyweight champ lived somewhere around here. Crenellated mansions loomed above precisely sculpted shrubbery and wrought-iron fencing, long rising carpets of bright green grass a half inch high, far off the road, winding stone driveways with their own street names, granite fountains. Private security cars patrolled the streets under arbors of live oak that flecked the pavement with sunshine.

The security cars were black with blue sirens on the roof, and they slowed as my truck passed.

I found the address and parked beneath a drooping oak. Some kids ran between sprinklers high up on one of the yards. It seemed like they should be in school. I wore my straw cowboy hat and sunglasses, and even with that shade the air so dazzled I had to squint.

Her house was a sierra of red brick and white shingles, columns framing the door. A garage off to the right was larger than the houses where I lived in Metairie. My JW was empty and I couldn't quite catch my breath.

Could you have lived here? I thought. Would you have ever known what to do with yourself?

I saw her move past a kitchen window and my throat narrowed.

Up close the brick of the house had a rosy tint, almost pink, and the paint on the shutters was precisely stripped to give an impression of antiquity. Ivy up the walls as neatly groomed as a professor's beard. My boots clunked and swerved up the pebbled driveway, which circled a stone birdbath big enough for two people.

A heavy, deep-stained door with a brass knocker in the shape of an eagle's head. I rapped with my fist. Never have used knockers.

Liquid courage, booze logic. I'd once heard that porpoises can commit suicide, but I don't know why that was on my mind.

Click of heels on tile. Sliding of locks, a creak. Loraine wore an accommodating face, a mask whose refinement made me feel a little subhuman just then, a little raw.

I took off my sunglasses. Twitches under my eye as I watched her expression fall and fade.

"Huh," she said. "I wondered."

She was no heavier but the skin of her neck was a little sun-creased, different shades in her hair, dyed the color of maples in October. Dark slacks fitted her hips and a white blouse poured down her like cream. A string of pearls and a large ring in addition to her wedding band and diamond. She ran the pearls between her fingers while she searched my face.

"You look completely different," she said.

"Hey, Loraine. Loraine. Hey."

Her eyes fell to my lips and then my stomach and back up to my own. Her cheeks had fallen some, I think, little pleats around her lips, and I wished that women would just ignore the urge to cut their hair short when they hit thirty.

"Roy. Well. Good God." She glanced behind her back as if someone else were there. "I told you I was busy."

"I only wanted to talk to you a second. I'll leave when you want."

"I told you I was busy."

"I'll stand out here."

"Well. What is it you want?"

141

"Talk," I muttered. "Catch up." I shrugged, as if it were a question.

She studied me with a mouth caught between annoyed and amused, and the sensation of her flesh came back to me as real as anything, the warmth under my fingers and the taste of her moistures, the narrowing of her waist and the way it spread out into her ass, the flush of her skin, like a map of blood when she was spent. Her toenails in the bathtub. Her face was wide and tapered at her chin, and I remembered how it looked turned up to the ceiling with a big smile, gasping. These things haunted my nerves like the twitching of an old injury or an illness that leaves you prone to chills.

She double-checked the yard, the neighbor's windows, and I thought I could almost smell the nape of her neck, a clean, citrus scent.

I could see her working out the easiest way to get rid of me. But I had some things to say. I was fairly drunk and I had things to say.

She laughed darkly. "Lord. Come on in, then. I don't want you standing on my porch, you goon." She opened the door and sighed. "It's just for a minute, though."

Inside, a long hallway stretched under a high ceiling, a wood floor so polished I could see myself all the way down in it, like water. Red and gold accents popped. As I walked behind her an inner tension unwound in me while my eyes soaked up the shape of her ass, my stomach unclenching at the memory of taking her from behind, keeping a thumb in that tiny hole the way she liked. It was more than the memory in my head, though. It was like my body remembered too, remembered by nearly feeling it again, the slippery grip of her, and I could almost taste her in my mouth. I lifted my thumb to my nose, half expecting the scent to be there.

A mirror with a gilded frame hung above a fine wood console, and little tables with jars or vases were set here and there, scarlet flowers. The hallway opened into a vaulted living room with a kind of small chandelier overhead, and to the left a staircase wound above the room. Thick couches in sand and earth colors, a pair of chocolate leather chairs. These things embarrassed me. When she turned, the look on her face embarrassed me.

I felt foolish, because I marked the soft white tablets of light that came down through the tall windows, facing out on a plush yard and pool, iron patio furniture, and I understood what she had always been on her way to being. How little I'd been a part of that.

"I guess you changed your mind about marriage."

"Well, you meet the right man." Her smile had bite in it, and she folded her arms at the threshold of the living room. "I don't really understand what you're doing here, I have to say."

I stared at her shoes. "I was just passing through. I've been—I mean, I was really just curious to hear how you've been."

"Been? Been since, what, eleven years ago?" She sat down in one of the leather chairs, crossed her legs, and rubbed her pearls between her fingers again. She cocked her head, some humor in this for her.

"Sure. How's the last eleven years been?"

"Let me see. Absolutely wonderful. There."

"You look good."

"When did you cut off all your hair?"

"Pretty recent."

"You know, you're not as handsome as I used to think."

"I actually get that a lot."

"You've kind of aged terribly."

"Wait'll it happens to you."

"Are you drunk?"

"Um. No." Heat flushed my face. She didn't believe me. I started thinking I might tell her about my lungs, earn some sympathy. Then I could say what I came here to say.

"Roy, you really can't stick around. I really am busy."

My fingers grazed the marble top of an end table. A savage piece of me thought of taking her, right there on the couch. Ask first, sure. But either way.

"I'm not staying," I said. "I'm going away."

"Well . . ."

"Do you—" I froze and handled a porcelain sculpture of clowns, put it down. "Do you remember when we went to Galveston for that one week? Seventy-six, I think."

She rolled her eyes in a tired way and looked a little bored. I remembered Nancy's face when Lance had tried nudging her down memory lane.

"I was thinking about it. On the beach. That was a good week. You told me about your sister, and your dad."

"Oh, Lord. You've gone sentimental, Roy. You're one of those nostalgic middle-aged men now." She shook her head with pity. "I'd rather you'd stayed the strong, silent type. I'd rather remember you like that."

"I'd just been thinking."

"Well. What did you imagine I'd say?"

I shrugged. I could hear the ticking of a grandfather clock in the corner, and it echoed quietly in the high room. A few pictures stood on an entertainment center. Her husband was thick-faced with thinning hair, a kind of friendly, pampered look to him, like a terrier.

"Do you have kids?"

She started fingering those pearls again. "What are you nostalgic about anyway? It didn't end good, Roy."

"Nothing does." But I wanted to answer her question by telling her how the dawn came into our windows at the place in Galveston, how the blue-white light had fallen over her in bed, sleeping on her stomach with no shirt, the sheets on the floor, and the smells of shrimp and salt on the cool Gulf breeze through the window, the sharp, sweet bite of those mojitos we'd lived on for the week, how *important* it seemed. How it was all intensely real to me now, how I could almost taste it and smell it and feel the ridges of her spine beneath my fingers.

I wouldn't, though. I knew it was stupid, a little pathetic that I'd never managed to make better memories.

I walked over to study the pictures by the big television. She and her husband posed on a white mountain, smiling in ski gear. The two of them toasting drinks on some beach far more blue and vivid than the Gulf.

"Has he ever heard about me?"

"Not much. But yes. He knows everything about me, Roy."

"I was thinking of a day. We were drunk on mojitos before noon. Scarfing crabmeat. We couldn't get the smell off. Laughing at ourselves, covered in crab juice. Drunk. Showering off."

"Okay, Tex. Simmer down, there."

"And later it rained and we stayed inside the next two days. Watched cable. All this unquenchable fucking."

"Yes, yes. I'm a dynamite piece of ass. Thank you, Roy."

I sat on the other chair, across from her. The leather squeaked if I moved an inch.

"I can't do this all day," she said.

I couldn't organize what I wanted to say. "It's just. I'm going away. Leaving the country. And it had gotten me thinking. There was a time—or like I've been *missing* something, now. I didn't *know*." I was painfully aware now of how drunk I'd gotten. Her face had slackened to a kind of distressed condolence, and it made me feel small. "I wanted to remember things again."

"Remember what, though? Remember being strung out? Remember watching you kick the shit out a poor cowboy who said *hi* to me? Remember drinking so much I threw up blood? This is what you're talking about to me. This is what I'm remembering."

"We had good—I *believe* we had good times."

"Oh. Oh, *Roy* . . ." She put a hand over her mouth and shook her head firmly. "I was *glad* when you went to prison, Roy."

I said, "My life is over."

She started looking around the room, like she was humiliated on my behalf.

"I told you about Port Arthur. The spades in high school. I told you about *me*."

She sighed, exasperated. "How'd you say you found me?"

"Clyde. In Beaumont. He said you were out here."

"How did he know?"

I shrugged.

"Christ. All my sins come back," she said.

The clock's ticking sounded like a woman in heels walking at a very slow and relentless pace across a marble floor.

"I have a meeting. I have Junior League, Roy."

"When we stayed up on the dunes that night."

"Oh, stop it. Really."

"How much we laughed—I can't remember. Do you remember what was so funny?"

"Get a grip, cowboy. Really. Locate a little dignity."

"For a while I was going to weld. You remember. I was going to leave the club, those guys. I remember wanting to do that. You didn't want me to. You liked that I did what I did."

"So what? I was a kid."

"All that *fucking*."

"Spare me."

"Hey. *You* were the one—"

"The past isn't real, Roy."

I stopped myself, caught on what she'd said.

"Listen to me," she said. "The past isn't real."

This struck the center of me like a pickax.

She said, "You remember what you want. I remember you coming home with your shirt bloody. Asking me to hide a gun. You'd sober up a week and start talking about being different. Then you were drunk again for three weeks straight. You made it so I couldn't be around you without being shit-faced. The things you said to me. You threw me around a little. Do you remember? Do you remember the fights at all? You were jealous of everything, Roy. You were resentful. You resented other people being happy. I remember thinking, *This is the most frightened man I ever met*. And so what, really? I've known worse men. I was a little relieved, though. When you went to prison."

"What did you ever like about me, then?"

Her fingernail tapped her chin. "I don't really remember. A kind of power, probably. But"—she sighed—"the kind that can only get you so far."

"There haven't been many like that. For me."

She put her head in her hand and half covered it. "I don't know what, in your mind, you've turned all this into. I was a stupid kid. That's all. I made mistakes. The tough guy. Oh, *that's* hot. I was stupid. A kid. I love my husband. My husband is a good man. I love my life with him."

Her scowl seemed baffled, no longer amused, and it stiffened all her beauty. Then she faced the window and the day outside reshaped her face in a softer way. I could feel the sensations that had skirted me fleeing. I tried to hold on to them by remembering us sitting cross-legged in bed, playing cards naked, but it didn't work, and I wanted to find a way to talk to her about time, how movement confuses you and wears you down, prevents things from sticking.

"What's he do?" I said. "Your husband."

"That's enough. I need you to get out of my house."

I stood up and walked over to her.

She looked up wearing a very bored, tired expression, and brandished a kind of garage door opener. "You see this, Roy? This sends an alarm to those Halliburton boys driving around out there."

I shrank. "Jesus. I was only going to say goodbye."

"Sure you were."

She followed me to the door, keeping a few paces behind. I opened it and stepped out, hammered by the light. On the porch I turned back to her.

"I'm dying," I said.

"Aren't we all."

The door thunked shut.

At the truck a hacking cough seized me and wouldn't subside. I retched as I started the engine, dropping a thin string of bile on the seat. I passed two security cars on my way to the interstate. I knew the past wasn't real. It was only an idea, and the thing I'd wanted to touch, to brush against, the feeling I couldn't name— it just didn't exist. It was only an idea, too.

I suppose you have to be very careful how you use your memories.

The thing was, once I admitted that to myself, everything that had ever happened to me still seemed important, more important, even. This is what you bought with your life.

I pulled onto the shoulder at the entrance to the freeway cloverleaf, and above me the concrete looped and knotted, the cars loud, wind whipping, white noise thickened with greasy exhaust and petrol fumes.

I thought about getting a room and whiskeying myself up. I could just drink and smoke in a motel room forever.

I had a strong taste of iron off the breeze, and it made me think of Matilda, the old black woman who cooked at the group home. Matilda was spiderlike, dark brown, and bent in her movements, her face like a walnut. She liked to stand in sunbeams and didn't give anything away about what she thought. She dipped tobacco that she cured herself and flavored with schnapps, made blood pudding with buckets of dark blood the hunters brought her as charity, men and their sons showing up with pails they'd drained from their kills, and I'd watch those men and think of the boys out with their fathers in the dark morning, the dew beads on the grass, stalking silent, following their fathers' backs. We ate a lot of blood pudding, and the taste, like iron shavings mixed with cornmeal, was heavy in my mouth just then, and I remembered the same taste and smell when I left the recruiting station and took the bus to Beaumont, remembered the taste had still been in my mouth when I found Robicheaux's-on-the-Bayou and asked for Harper Robicheaux.

I felt along my mouth with my tongue and watched the passing cars enter the freeway, and the gamy taste brought with it the heavy feelings of sunlight on my skin, the layers and layers of lush greenery, the soft chirring sounds that were part of the silence, the silence in the cotton fields, the briars cutting your hands, long days spent hunched and picking, blind with dirty sweat.

Tiffany's laughter pealed through my head, those sounds she made as I tossed her into the waves. And Rocky's face, distressed, recalled a badly staked tent in a shuddering gale.

A dragonfly kept circling my head as if it had something to tell me, and the air of the hot night was like breathing ashes. In the distance I could hear the cars pass *whoosh–whoosh–whoosh* like the great heartbeat of some huge animal that had swallowed me.

Amarillo was gas stations and storage units, low-end strip clubs between motels, pounding winds. You could drive and drive but there would still be only the plains and the water towers and the small derricks bobbing up and down like seesaws. I watched truckers and bathroom whores trudge through the drizzle, moving between the laundromat and the service station where the big rigs sat in rows under halogen lamps. A woman with real tall hair climbed out one truck and got into another right next to it. The girl in my room made a contrite, apologetic face while I stood at the window. She was on the bed and I could see her in the glass.

"What's wrong, mister? Tell me what to do. You tell me what you want."

Her pale face and ink black hair floated in the glass. I was naked beside the curtains and watching the parking lot. I sipped JW.

When I didn't answer her, she said, "You're just drunk, baby."

I hadn't planned on meeting her, but the night found me in Amarillo after a day of driving in the wrong direction. An outpost of bright lights, a truck stop more like a small village, had a laundromat and bar posted beside it, and facing it across the giant lot a short motel of single rooms squatted.

I'd walked into the bar first, but the tinsel around the bottle island looked too gaudy and the slope-eye of the waitress came out of the shadows like an anglerfish materializing from the darkest part of the ocean. Static filled the television's noise, and the voices from it sounded like endless newspapers being crushed. The bartender's jaw hung slack and he turned to look at me with an evil blue light flickering across his face, which seemed without thought. There was no one drinking in the bar.

I walked out and into a drizzle's steady pour. Men in adjustable caps were towed back and forth by their bouldery guts. I passed the laundromat and saw the girl. She was young, hard to say her age, but she watched me through the glass and followed me with her eyes. She stood against a machine with her arms folded and her neck craned out, watching me in this posture like a mantis, with the light rain flowing over the window, and I had this feeling of a great tribunal pointing its fingers at me.

A rear portion of the service station had a doughnut shop inside, with booths and a few tables, and this was the place some men gathered. Large men shaped like pinecones, pants hung low off assless waists, overalls, denim. Aviator shades at night. They looked at me when I came in. Nobody was laughing, but they talked quietly and seriously and made little gestures with their cigarettes to drive home a point. Some stuck to their coffee and cigarettes and a few others passed around a pint of bourbon. The ones that weren't sharing the bourbon kept dipping their paws in a box of crullers.

For a while I just stood in one of the aisles, with potato chips and jerky on my left and rows of single-serving medicine on my right. The harsh lights were like moonlight, only brighter. I kept seeing the men in the doughnut shop look over at me. The woman behind the counter wished me ill. The girl appeared outside then, on the other side of the window, and her eyes burned at me through the sliding water. She wasn't going to let me get away. She'd ask me for money. That's how it works. All they have to do is make eye contact.

But I looked up at the men in the doughnut shop and the fat woman scowling at me from behind the counter, and I felt the heavy, damp air of the bar blow over me again, and when I walked outside she was waiting for me. I stood beside her awhile, and we stared at each other.

"You want to buy some?" she said.

I asked her if she had a room, and she said no.

"You got a manager?"

She shook her head and folded her arms tighter. The rain was quitting, and her neck craned out into it.

"It's just me," she said. "What do you think?"

A runaway. She wouldn't be doing this long, between the pimps and psychos and cops. I pulled out my flask and took a hit, passed it to her. We watched the men moving around the pumps and the occasional woman step down from one of the parked rigs. A lot of times they run off and don't understand where they are. Then they run back home, if they can. But it's too late.

I looked her over again and wondered why her neck bowed like that. She had a bony face and her eyes were a little too close together and too large, insectlike, an impression of malnourishment in her skin. But she had strong shoulders and a nice body in a denim skirt with red tights and a black top, a large floppy purse hugged to her hip like an infant. She pulled some of her wet, utterly black hair off her forehead. "Come on," she said.

"All right," I said. "Follow me."

It turned out I didn't want her at all. I just hadn't wanted to be alone. I tried conversing, tried to talk about things. But she was too much of a whore, wouldn't even speak, just kept making for my pants. She was younger than I'd thought, too. After a while, when I was pissed off and she was embarrassed, I went back to my drink and stood naked near the window. The rain had started again.

"Just tell me what you want," she said.

"How long you been working these parts?" I wasn't sure where that question came from. I wouldn't have asked a week ago.

I saw her stretch out on the bed, and in the glass her curving whiteness resembled smoke. "A couple days. I was sleeping on my feet yesterday."

"The girls out here are dangerous. They'll cut you. Their men will."

She folded the covers over her. "I'm not staying here. I'm going west."

The reflection of my face out of the black night mingled with hers and overlaid the things past the window.

"You might find the same thing out west," I said.

"I don't do charity," she said. "I earn my way. Come back here and tell me what you want."

When I didn't move or answer she rolled over and curled up, pulling the covers tight. There was nothing in her to remind me of Loraine or Carmen, just a kid and frightened by where she'd run to. The rain tapping delicately at the roof and weeping down the window made me feel mean, and I knew this girl would never make it. I could see her life unspool. I got dressed, started to step outside, and she snapped at me without turning over. "Just *pay* me."

I left some bills on the air conditioner and went out to my truck. I pulled away and left her the room, if she wanted it.

You're born and forty years later you hobble out a bar, startled by your own aches. Nobody knows you. You steer down lightless highways, and you invent a destination because movement is key. So you head toward the last thing you have left to lose, with no real idea what you're going to do with it.

FOUR

Strips of sand wriggle across the street with the movements of sidewinders. Sage sits straight and alert as we wait for traffic to pass, cut through the parking lot of a day care and cross Pabst Road to the Knight's Arms. Cecil rents rooms here at a weekly rate, and a consolation of staying in this place is the reassurance that you won't be here long.

I've lived here five years, in an efficiency with a small couch that unfolds into a double bed. My television died a couple months ago, and books pile atop themselves along most of the wall, stacked on their sides like bricks, the way I learned to keep my books in prison, so you don't need shelves.

I drop the sack in the sink and feed Sage. When she's done eating she curls on her pillow beside the couch, and I'm still thinking about the man in the Jaguar, if he's alone or if he brought friends with him. I turn up the wall unit and switch off the lights, and by nine thirty I'm in the management office.

Cecil is looking through the Life section of *USA Today*. He's been living in the office since his divorce, but now his ex-wife's moved to Austin and his house is free. Only now he's thinking he'll rent the house and keep living in the office until he meets another girl. I'm supposed to paint that house today.

He's more than twenty years younger than me and the edge of a black tattoo peeks out from the back of his collar. He made some money in Washington State in the late nineties and moved here with his girl for the weather. The girl became his wife and then she left him for a DJ in Austin, and now he says they should have gone to Florida.

When he hired me in spite of the prison record, he said, "Tell you the truth, I didn't think I'd find a guy that spoke English." He wanted a man living on the grounds, so the position includes the efficiency, even though he's living here now and doesn't need me as much. He also lets me keep Sage when the motel policy is no pets. So I think of him as a decent guy.

He chews his sunken cheek and says, "You seen what's happening with the hurricane?"

"Like every other September. You can't ever tell what they're going to do."

"I guess. They're talking state of emergency now. Mandatory evacuation in the next day or two, maybe."

"Right when everybody leaves, it'll turn into a squall off Padre Island."

"It still freaks me out. Ever since New Orleans."

"Listen." I lean on the counter. "That note you left on my door."

"Yeah. That guy catch up to you?"

"No. Tell me about him."

"Sort of official-looking. Guy in a suit, professional type. Gruff. Asked if you were around. Told me your name. Asked if Roy Cady works here."

The metal in my skull throbs, and all the morning's disjointed thoughts come together in a siren sound rising in my head. "I was at the Seahorse. I cut out early."

"Figured something like that. I didn't say anything, though. I didn't know. Guy didn't want to leave a message, either. I didn't like that."

He slides the house keys over to me. "There's a hole in the hallway wall you could patch up for me, if you feel like it," he says. His brown hair is going too thin for him to keep wearing it spiky like that, and the bags under his eyes make him look older than he is. "Paint's all in the truck. Bought some spackle, too, if you want to fix that hole. I'd appreciate it."

"Sure thing."

"I wondered about that guy," he says, folding the paper shut. "Something off about him. A collection agency maybe? Lawyers get guys like that. So I didn't tell him where you might be."

"I don't owe anybody money."

"Hey, good for you." He switches on the television behind the counter.

But I do owe things.

"What did he look like?" I ask.

"Like I said. Sort of a thick guy. Hair slicked back. Sort of tough-looking about it. You want me to tell him anything, if he comes back?"

"Did he say he'd be back?"

"When I asked if he wanted to leave a message, he just said he'd try back. I didn't like that. The dude's whole demeanor."

"Don't tell him anything."

He's watching the weather report on television and scratches his weak chin. I take the keys and turn to leave, but stop myself.

"Tell him I'm not around. Even if I am. Just tell me if he comes back. Try to get a name again."

"He anybody you know?"

"I got no idea who he could be."

"All right. Remember the hole in the hallway, huh?"

I leave him and walk to the storage shed, haul out two big plastic tarps, rollers, mixing pans, and bring them to Cecil's truck. He's letting me borrow it to paint the house. I'm thinking about bagmen and skip tracers, the man in the Jaguar talking on a cell phone, telling his bosses he found me, and I wonder again if they're sending anyone else.

Before I leave I turn on the hose in the courtyard. It has a spray-gun fixture at its end, and the sight of it in my palm sends a ripple of dread down my spine.

Both hands shaking.

I lean behind the shed and smoke half a joint, hoping it will settle me and not fire up the paranoia. It ends up doing both, making me certain of my doom, which will be painful and humiliating, but also giving me a kind of Zen outlook on the inevitability of suffering.

I should buy a gun, maybe.

Upstairs I dig in my closet until I find the Remington hunting knife I won at cards a few years ago, a seven-inch blade with a serrated base. I run my thumb along the edge. It's a little dull and I take the sharpening stone from the sheath, file the blade until with no pressure it draws blood from my thumb. I put the knife in one of the pockets of my overalls, check the parking lot for black Jaguars, and climb down.

I drive Cecil's truck out of Spanish Grant and past the beaches to Point San Luis on the far west end. I pass Lafitte's

Cove and imagine the evil bravery of that time, the fires on the beaches. And I remember Rocky, of course.

Driving, this might be the farthest I've traveled in five years. Except for the odd nights at Finest Donuts or the Seahorse, when I need to be around people so I won't go buy that final bottle, I usually stay inside. Even during the hurricane evacuations I've seen here, I've stayed home and watched the storms whip the air with leaves and rain. I squash the thought of taking Cecil's truck up to Montana or Wyoming, maybe Alaska.

I suppose that's when I admit to myself that I'm not going to run.

Cecil's house is a bungalow on a raised foundation, painted a dull wheat color, and the yard is wild and overgrown. Between my hands and the bum leg, it takes a few minutes for me to bring all the supplies inside. The house is empty and all the curtains gone, so the light pours in through the windows in huge slabs of chalky white.

I lay down the tarp and unfold the newspapers, tape the wainscot in the living room. These rooms have a strange feeling, being empty and with all that powdery light pouring in. Such white and bereft light. It's definitely a house, a place too big for one person. Families have moved through this space. I walk around, my left foot making a sandy sound scraping across the floor, and I pass through all these crosshairs of sunshine. I'm thinking about things I've read about this or that great painter. How the quality of light changes everything—not only what you see but how you *feel* about what you see.

I've read that certain stroke victims see a ferocious white light, a light that comes from inside their brains.

That's how I would describe the brightness in these empty rooms.

All day I wait for them. Every time a car door slams I grip the knife in my overalls, and when the day is done I circle the Knight's Arms, scouting for the black Jaguar, then I unload the paint supplies, give Cecil back his keys, and climb up to my apartment.

As always it's a small struggle to get my overalls off because my left knee doesn't like to bend. I smoke the second half of my day's joint, then I slip on a windbreaker and leave to take Sage to the beach.

I stop halfway down the stairs and go back for the hunting knife.

Only a few people are out on the sand, what with these skies. A couple of them glance toward me, then turn away. I toss Sage's giraffe into the breakers and she leaps after it. Some kids laugh and follow her as she runs back up the shore to my feet. The children stop running when they see me. The sun is behind us now, and the air has lost its burn. The three kids stare up from the bottom of a dune, watching Sage and glancing at me. I suppose they're trying to decide if Sage is worth having to talk to me.

The smallest, a straw-colored boy, calls up, "What's your dog's name?"

"Sage."

"Does he bite?"

"It's a girl," I say. "Sometimes she bites. Sometimes she doesn't."

He looks at his friends and starts up the dune. The other two, a boy and girl, both taller and older than him, follow warily. People are leaving the beach, packing bags and dumping their children's sand-castle molds. The children crouch around Sage, who spins from one to the other while they all try to pet her at the same time. I watch the children laugh and grip the knife in my pocket, squeeze the handle so it won't slip out my jacket. The blond boy says, "What happened to your eye?"

"*Sutton!*" The girl says. "That's so *rude*."

I grin at her, thinking of another child. "It's all right," I say. "It was an accident. A long time ago."

"Is that what happened to your face?"

"*Sutton!*" The girl starts trying to capture Sage in a hug, but the dog wriggles out beneath her.

"It was the same accident, yes."

"Did it hurt?" the boy asks.

I tell him, "I don't remember."

complete two circuits around the Knight's Arms, starting three blocks away and moving closer in concentric circles, checking the street and parking lots for the Jaguar, for men in luxury cars, men wearing sunglasses, anybody watching the place. The hotel has walls of beige stucco, the bottom floors raised on a brick foundation. In the apartment I untie the canvas sack in the sink, dump that morning's crabs into boiling water, and the trapped air of their shells shrieks like tiny human voices.

When they're done I turn off the stove, but I'm not hungry. I eat less and less these days. I just don't seem to need it.

I roll another joint and pick up a novel about mountain climbers. When it worked, reading could take away the burden of time.

This reading habit I picked up over the last twenty years doesn't make me a different person. It just became the best way for me to spend time, since I couldn't drink.

But it doesn't work tonight. Tonight the book makes me remember more, not less. I recall the feel of Rocky's back as we danced at that cowboy joint in Angleton, the lights on the dance floor. I finish my joint and throw one of the crabs into Sage's bowl. I can hear the hot wind blowing hard outside, the ocean growling.

I think of the man in the Jaguar and with all my heart I hope for the worst. I put on my jacket, slip the hunting knife into my boot.

The Seahorse keeps regulars who mostly work trade jobs, belong to unions, and some old fishermen too, salt-red shrimpers and net haulers and their women hunch around tables made of cable spools, nets hung from rafters, an alligator's skull wearing sunglasses, and a giant garfish monstrosity stretched about nine feet along the back wall. People drop peanuts or crawfish heads for the blond Labrador that rouses from under the pool tables to circle their stools when someone orders food. It smells like red pepper and fish and beer, like sawdust and too much perfume. The lamps in the Seahorse are behind prism-cut portholes that portion the light into stained fragments that lie over things. The boys from Finest Donuts don't come in so as not to invite temptation, but it's only a block away and I sometimes enjoy getting high and coming to sit at the end of the bar with a glass of milk and my Camels. Everyone who comes here is poor and a liar.

"Skim or whole?" Sara asks.

"Whole. Come on."

She makes a face like I think I'm hoity-toity. She's here six nights a week, moving those thick arms between the cooler and bar, pinching her lips at the stories people tell, picking on the old men who sit here all day drinking.

The faces along the rail turn to shadow or become oddly poignant, gazing up into the pale blue light of the television that sits behind the bar. The television shows a computerized weather map, and just beyond the Texas coast, in the Gulf of Mexico, a bright swirl of red and purple revolves, like the thumbprint of God, come to lay His finger down. Everyone's talking about it.

"Could be real bad."

"It won't come here."

"It might."

"Nowhere near. I got a hundred bucks. Put a hundred on it."

"Fuck you. 'A hundred.' What a thing to say to me."

The storm's closer than anyone wants to admit, though. Ike, they're calling this one. The screws in my bones tingle, and pretty soon the pressure behind my eyes is too much, so I'm ready to leave.

I pause at the door. I can see him through the barred window.

A black Jaguar, the windows lightless, sits between a Ford truck and a little Jap model, facing the bar. A man in a suit climbs out. He's big, and I guess he's not going to wait for me to come out this time.

So I trudge backward and down the hall where the bathrooms are, to the back exit. I push through and walk east for two blocks, circle back, and position myself behind an old phone booth, and I watch the car in the Seahorse's lot. A truck enters the lot and when its lights pass over I see that the Jaguar is empty.

I crouch, slip the knife out my boot and hide it under the front of my jacket.

I start to turn to take the long way around to the Knight's Arms. I could throw together a bag and grab Sage and get us both on a bus to Carson City, Eureka Springs, Billings. But watching the car, I know that won't happen. I feel a kind of impatience well up, and my sense of offense starts riling.

Well, let it come down. Let's get it all out in the open. All at once I become pretty jacked at the idea of a quick death earned in a final stand. I start walking back to the car.

I approach from the rear, creeping up to its trunk. My nerves jangle, heart like a paint mixer, and I crouch beside the back door on the driver's side. I try the door, and when the handle gives I open it quick and throw myself in. I scan for some clue, but the car's clean except for the queasy stench of cologne. So I lie down and watch. It's not long before the man exits the bar, looks around the lot. When he comes back and sits down, I've got the tip of my knife at the back of his neck as he sticks in the key.

"Jesus—"

"Turn around. Put your hands up on the steering wheel."

He does, wrapping meaty paws around the wheel, a couple gold rings gilding his knuckles, and the hair at the back of his head is trimmed in a straight line. He's got some size to him, and the ripe, oversweet smell of his cologne fills the cabin. I snort. "You guidos and your beauty supplies."

The car is well kept, lit only by the green glow of the instrument panel, sleek leather, and the radio is broadcasting an exhibition game. I lean toward his face, examining it by the dash lights. A plump, square face, a natural kind of arrogance in its snarl. He's no one I recognize.

"You're looking for someone," I say. "Don't turn around."

"Roy Cady?"

"Shut up." I press the knife at his neck and he yelps. "I have a message for you. Tell them to come get me."

"Wait a minute."

"Shut up." He winces and a teardrop of blood pools beneath

the knife's tip. "Don't talk, bagman. All you have to do is take a message. You tell them to come on. I'm right here, and I will burn their fucking lives to the ground." I don't think he can hear the tremble in my voice, and I squeeze the knife handle to keep from shaking.

"Tell them I'm waiting. Tell them to get the show on the road."

"Wait—"

I don't want to hear it, and press the knife so that he shuts up. I'm suffocating in this rich vehicle and its cloud of cologne. "Tell them what I said." My other hand releases the door handle. "If I see you again I'm going to blow your teeth out the back of your head and claim self-defense."

I jump out the car and hobble as quick as I can into the shadows, and the man in the car calls out to me, but whatever he says is lost on the wind. My ribs ache from my heart's kicking, and the metal in my eye socket throbs. I stick to the shadows and alleys, moving quickly through the light, and when I reach the Knight's Arms the Jaguar hasn't gotten there yet.

I shudder up the stairs and slam the door behind me. Decimated crab shell covers the floor in the kitchenette and the place smells like the docks. I dump my jacket and fall on the couch, keeping the lights off. Sage looks up from her bed and whines. She assumes I'm upset about the mess she made, and I scratch her ear to reassure her.

The only light comes from above the oven in the kitchenette, and I sit on my couch, staring at the dead gray face of the TV and the wall of stacked books, my thumb running back and forth over the edge of the knife, each time cutting a little deeper. I didn't hear what the man shouted at me.

I take out my bridges and set the teeth floating in a glass of mint mouthwash. I watch them for a while, and they are like the intrusion of a ghost.

I sit rigid on the couch, idly scrape the bottom of my jaw with the knife.

I watch the door. They'll kick open the door, when they come. My thumb is bleeding.

FIVE

I arrived back to the island on a Thursday, a little past noon, three days after I'd left. The police tape had been taken off the door to number 2, and a cleaning woman's cart stood on the walkway between rooms. The station wagon was gone and the kid's motorcycle still perched in front his room. Some seagulls strutted the parking lot with a kind of haughty entitlement that made me think of clergy.

Nobody answered the door to Rocky and Tiffany's room.

My stomach had the heavy, sickly feeling that made my back grow hot and my thoughts speed up. I walked across the parking lot and when I opened the door to the office I heard a trilling sort of song. Around the corner cartoon animals sang on the television while building a dress, little birds looping ribbons around a princess. Nonie and Dehra and Nancy were there, and Tiffany sat on the floor eating a bowl of cereal and giggling.

All the women looked up at me.

"Hi there," said Nancy, without warmth.

"Hello," said Dehra, and her sister nodded.

They didn't turn back to the television, just watched me. Tiffany saw me and waved her hand, went back to the cartoon. Her clothes looked new, a bright white jumpsuit.

"We've watched this about ten times," said Dehra. The sisters chuckled, but it sounded manufactured and that made the sense of wrong hang in the air. I guess I didn't look too good, red eyes, a sapped complexion.

I asked Nancy, "Where's Rocky?"

The sisters returned their attention to the TV. Nancy's eyes narrowed on me like blades.

"She *said* she's at work. She hasn't been around much the last couple days. Thought you knew."

I held myself up with the counter, shook my head. "I was visiting old friends. She got a job?"

She turned away and took some time to answer. "I think there was some confusion about whether you'd be back."

"Of course I would. I'm paid up for more days. How's the kid?"

"A *doll*," said Dehra.

Nancy said, "She's precious. She's a darling. And she deserves better than this."

"Agreed," I said.

Nancy stopped herself from saying more just then, and we both watched Tiffany wipe her mouth and rise sleepily, crawl into Nonie's lap and yawn. Nancy rose off the couch and moved around the counter. She spoke low and sharply. "Come here."

I followed her outside and we stood under the carport's shade. I glanced at Tray's room; the curtains were closed behind the squares of mashed foil.

Nancy's jaw flexed. She scrutinized my face as if I might have robbed her. "Just to say," she said, "what that girl's up to? I don't need none of that around here. Don't need it. Won't abide it."

"I don't follow."

"She had a man in her room. Night you left. Okay. No big deal. Her business." She stroked the inside of her elbow with her nails. "But yesterday, Lance comes to me apologizing. Tells me she offered him a good rate. Says he's apologizing because he loves me and didn't mean to, but he's weak. All that bullshit." Her lips had become a bloodless slash and her eyes probed hard at mine.

"Nancy, I don't know about any of this."

"Really? 'Cause if you don't know about it, then who does? I mean, I can't exactly understand what kind of arrangement you got with that girl—don't want to understand it, frankly—but I do know she's not your niece. And that little one inside there? That's a special little person. And she deserves way better than this here, Mr. Robicheaux."

She jerked her head toward the office. "That little one don't need to turn out like the other."

"What happened? After you talked to Lance?"

"We're not doing it for her, you understand. Or you either. Normally I'd toss her ass out. Called the sheriff's, too, maybe. But I didn't. And the reason I didn't is for that little one in there."

"But what happened? After?"

She tugged one of her earrings. "Well, I go to talk to her. She's angry and yelling, storms into her room. Comes out in a little dress, with her hair kind of done up, and she brings the little one out and knocks on Nonie and Dee's door, asks them to watch her because she has to go to work. Got a job. I'm watching all this, 'cause I'm also watching Lance pack up his things."

"Where does she work?"

"Supposedly, this restaurant on the Strand. Pirandello's. Italian place. Says she's a hostess. I seen her hanging around the Jones man in number eight, too. Seen them drinking. He gave her the ride to work. You know, that girl can't wear heels at all—somebody ought tell her not to wear them. She tried to give me a mean stare on her way out, but mine was bigger. Off she goes. We haven't seen her since. Nonie and Dee, you understand, they're happy as can be to watch the little one. I think they're hoping they can just keep watching her. But after what happened with that family in number two—? Well. I'm more inclined to take an interest in what's going on around here."

"Shit." I fumbled with how to convince her I wasn't the sort of man who'd go along with this type of thing. My throat was dry and my eyeballs cramped.

"Shit is right, Mr. Robicheaux. Now. You know I could call social service? I could tell them this little one's been abandoned. I could say her sister or whoever was tricking, and they'd lock that girl up. I could say, that one there, the big mean-looking drunkard, he's her pimp."

"That's not true."

"Which part? What do I know? I'm just telling you I could of done it. Called somebody. You know why I didn't."

"Yeah."

"Yeah. That little one in there."

"I didn't know about any of this. I swear."

She stretched to my face. "Who *are* you?"

I pulled a cigarette and she refused one. I lit mine and leaned against the wall, and the glare was giving me a headache.

"She's a girl I helped out a bad spot. We were both in a bad spot, tell you the truth. I didn't know her. She wanted a ride to Texas for her and her little sister. I ended up sticking around kind of, don't know why. I guess I wanted to keep an eye on them for a while. I don't know."

"Good job doing that."

"Well, listen. However bad you think that baby's got it here, I guarantee you where she was from—the situation she was in? That was way worse. I seen the house she came from."

"Mm. I can believe that." She looked down at my boots and rubbed her arms. "She flinches if you move too fast around her. You seen that? She's jumpy."

"Yeah. I saw it when we played on the beach."

"Look here in my eyes, Mr. Robicheaux." I did. "Are you that girl's pimp or something like it?"

"No. No, ma'am, I'm not. Nothing like it. I just tried to help her out a little and it's brought me here."

"Mm." She fixed that icy judgment on me, the creased breakage of her face, recriminating. My headache had started pulsing and I reminded myself that I didn't allow people to talk to me this way.

"What'd you like me to do? *Huh?* How about I jump in my truck and leave them both here? They're *not* my problem. You understand? Hell—*I'll* call social services for you. Let *me* do it. They'll take the little one away. They'd get her a foster. Then I don't have to think about any of this shit anymore. How about *I* say there's this crazy kid I gave a ride to and she abandoned her little sister with me?"

She crossed her arms and pointed her chin up, and she didn't move an inch back when I crowded her.

179

"I think you wouldn't like to talk to the sheriff's about much of anything. I heard her call you 'Roy' once. I'm thinking your name isn't even real, and you sure as *hell* don't want nobody taking your fingerprints."

I whipped the cigarette out my mouth and a gull hopped to dodge the burst of sparks.

"Maybe I'll just take off, then. You can get Rocky put in jail and the girl with a foster, and none of it's got jack shit to do with me."

"I guess you could do that. But I think you already could of done that. If you were going to. Maybe you tried that already. And it didn't work."

I glanced around the motel.

"You don't want to leave her either," she said. "You like that little one, too."

I rubbed my eyes and held my palms up. "All right. Let's stop bullshitting each other."

She laughed a little, not entirely out of spite. "We can. But let me say. Whatever's coming, that little girl's going to need taking care of."

I nodded. We leaned against the wall and watched the birds in the lot. The warm wind shushed between buildings, and drifts of sand washed across the concrete. The air was so thick with ocean I could taste algae.

"Well?" she said.

"Can you watch that little girl a while longer? I'm going to find where Rocky is. Okay?"

She thought. "How long?"

"Not long."

I walked to number 8, and at the door I turned and saw that

Nancy still watched me. I waited until she went back inside and knocked.

He checked the peephole first, winced when he opened the door to a sliver of sunlight. I pushed inside and shut the door. He was shirtless and swaybacked, his skinny arms dangling like deadweight. It was dark inside and heavy with cigarette smoke, body odor—sweats.

"Hey, cowboy," Tray mumbled, then dropped onto his bed. He spread his arms and stared up at the ceiling. A sheen of perspiration covered his face and his eyelids fluttered. Drifting. High. Skinny as Christ.

"You know where Rocky is?"

He spoke slowly. "Said . . . she's gone to work."

"What happened with you and her?"

"Happened?" He sat up, rubbed his face. I could see his ribs and the striations of his thin muscles. "Nothing happened, man. We hung out. Drank some beer. I gave her a ride to work."

"You pay her?"

"What? Man"—he shook his head, chuckled—"the Killer isn't into the *chickens*. You dig?"

I stepped up and crowded him at the edge of the bed. "Where'd you take her?"

He kept his head facing the floor, arms slack between his legs. "Um, down the Strand. Just let her off."

His garbage bag of clothes had spilled across the carpet, and I noticed the books on his table were open, those drawings spread around the room.

I almost left, but I stopped. "Where'd you cop?" I said.

"What?"

"Where'd you get the drugs? You looked clean before."

"Oh. You know. It's around if you want it."

"You come into some cash?"

Lazy eyes rolled up to me, and he grinned with a shrug. "You thought any more about what we talked about?"

"No. Not interested."

"Huh." He rolled away so that he could stand up. Dug in the garbage bag and pulled out a T-shirt for himself, then walked to the sink and splashed water over his face, ran wet hands through his hair and finger-combed it straight.

"Saw you leave," he said.

I watched him put on a pair of tennis shoes and dig around his papers for a cigarette. He lit it, turned on a lamp, and sat down, let the smoke float out like he had nothing but time. His voice had turned sober, and that Texas accent had almost disappeared completely. "Saw you jump up with that paper in your hands. I was right there. At the peephole. Saw you toss it and make tracks."

My chest became heavy, that feeling of insides hardening like concrete.

"Found it in the trash. I's just reading along, realized, hey—them girls in that article got the same name as these girls here. One plus one, you know. Pretty simple."

My teeth squeaked, clenching, and my fists curled. He didn't seem to notice.

He held up a hand. "None of my business, man. I ain't got *no* desire to screw you any way, shape, or form. Just saying. If it comes to that."

"Comes to what?" I said.

He leaned forward. He slid the ashtray over on the table

and trimmed the cherry of his cigarette by rolling it across the grooved plastic edge.

"You know, working without a partner here, there's a better chance I'm gonna get busted. If not the cops, then somebody else. You feel me? So, you know, look at it this way. You feature me in bracelets at some point, sweating some police box. I'm losing it, you know, getting sick, just needing out. And the cops, these asshole hard-liners, are loving it. This cop wants me down for a long stretch. He wants to kill my future. So I'm desperate, sick, freaking out. I might could get weak. I could say, 'Listen, you all give me some flex, some pull, you all forget the charges and I can give you a murder. I can tell you something about some missing girls.'"

My knuckles throbbed and blood pressed up behind my eyes. Then he started playing with a butterfly knife he'd slipped from under some papers. He flipped it around and upside down and let the little blade flash in his hand. This was meant to announce that he could take care of himself, and he picked his teeth with the blade to show how he took it all in stride.

"Just think it over, man. I'm saying, I got no desire to screw you up. I'm saying, *let's make some money*. Help me, help you. There's a fifteen thousand payout for you at the end. *Let's make some money*." I could hear the vibrato skip under his voice now and then, and the pitch of it rose a little bit, and he kept looking at things on the table, lacing up his shoes, keeping away from my eyes. "Or else we both take our chances."

I stared, my worst umbrage subdued because I almost felt sorry for him. He hadn't been taught good enough. He didn't know me or what telling me these things meant for him. He tapped his smoke a little, straightened his jeans and scratched his arm, stroked his hair, and when there was nowhere else left to look, he faced me. His eye twitched.

I said, "This is it, though? I do the one thing with you, how do I know you're not holding this over my head? How do I know you won't want to do it all over again? Like you won't put me on a leash."

"Aw, man. That's what I'm trying to say. It's not about that. I *ain't* about that. This is an exchange of favors. One for one. Even up."

I noticed a barely visible line of red ants stringing along the baseboard of the room, and my sight roamed the papers on the table, little maps and circuit diagrams. A lot of the doodles were types of pentagrams, sketches of goat heads and butterfly knives.

He said, "I guess you just have to trust me, man. But I'm straight. I don't say one thing and do the other. Just take a look at it, man. Hear me out. Just take a look at what I got set up, listen to what I got to say. Take a look."

We sat there a moment and I could feel the heat ease off the aluminum foil at the window, and somehow I could tell it had darkened outside, like cloud cover had docked above us.

"All right," I said. "It's going to wait till dark, though. I have to go see about finding Rocky."

"Yes. All right. I'm telling you." He looked less like a kid when he smiled—his face wrinkled up and those crooked little teeth flashed like a handful of pebbles.

I stood up. "Probably people around here shouldn't see us hanging out together. Meet me at that Circle K down the block. Eight o'clock."

"You're paranoid, brah. Ain't nobody here going to know anything."

"You want me in, we're going to start being careful. Right now."

"Okay, okay. Man, you remind me of Wilson that way."

"Then do what I say."

He aye-ayed me with a mock salute. I didn't look back as I walked out the room. I saw that I'd been right: furrows of gray clouds had piled up and hung down low, as if the crowded sky pressing down on us was the underside of a mountain.

I found the restaurant on Twenty-second between Ship's Mechanic Row and Market Street. Pirandello's was the bottom floor of a brownstone, and an arrangement of lightbulbs encased in glass flumes, shaped like flames, framed the entrance. Cursive script scrawled across the glass door, and burgundy curtains draped over the top halves of the windows. Down the sidewalk a man was yelling at a dog.

A hostess met me as soon as I entered. The staff wore black pants or skirts with white dress shirts and black bow ties. It was five o'clock and she told me the kitchen had just opened, asked if I wanted a table. The dining area was about a third full with women wearing blouses and jewelry, sporting big Texas hair.

"Is Rocky working now?"

"Who?"

"Rocky. Or Raquel? Small girl, has short blond hair. Real blond."

Her face scrunched, thinking it over, and she looked down at the seating chart. "I don't think I know her."

"She doesn't work here?"

"I've only been here a few weeks. I guess there might be some people I don't know yet."

"You know the other hostesses, though? You never seen this girl—real petite, with kind of feathery hair, really pretty. Small."

"You know. I think I seen a girl like that at the bar once or twice. I didn't think she worked here." She motioned behind her, past the waiting area and the main floor, where a long, ritzy bar rail set at the end of the dining room was tended by a man in shirtsleeves and the kind of elbow garters men wore back in the last century or sometime.

He looked about my age, tanned the color of delta mud, and pale eyebrows were almost lost in his skin when he glanced up at me. He nodded, fixing with precise movements some drinks for a waitress. In any occupation you can usually judge a man's professionalism by the way he uses his hands, whether he moves them loosely or in tight, controlled gestures. He greeted me and I ordered a Miller, tipped him equal to its price.

"Thanks." He nodded. "Meeting somebody?"

"Actually, I'm looking for a girl. I kind of thought she worked here."

I described Rocky again and called her Raquel again. "You know her? This short blond hair, lemon-colored. Sharp face, pretty. Told me she worked here."

His eyebrows raised and his sun-beaten skin paled in stripes across his brow. He petted a neatly trimmed goatee. "I think I might know who you mean, man. She don't work here, though. She come in the bar a couple times, right there. Sat around till somebody joined her. She'd sit here smoking till somebody offered her a drink."

"Really?"

He nodded and looked a little amused. "You looking for company, I know a few girls. I could make a call for you, you want."

"Just the one."

"Well. She's in here twice that I know of. I was told by management to say something if she comes back. This is kind of a classy place, you know."

My eyes scanned the sponge-painted walls papered with shreds of gold leaf, the paper-mache sculptures of the Coliseum, the leaning tower.

"I mean, people's business is their own. But she should try one of the hotel bars or something. This isn't the place for it."

"All right." I rose off my stool and tossed him an extra five for the conversation. It was no trouble to picture Rocky walking in there the first time, and maybe she hadn't even filled out an application, but sat in the bar, alone. Somebody approaches her, or she tosses a look, because she knows how to do that, and a few hours later she's back at the motel, has money, and tells everybody she found a job.

I cruised Harborside and down Rosenberg Avenue and toward Seawall, crawled along the beach and the people crowding one another in dusky gray sands, the sun setting the edges of everything afire and coming through the windshield in thick red wavelengths. I kept my eyes peeled for that bright shade of hair. A man had his legs bent on a bus bench, newspaper folded over his face, and women in bikini tops moved in and out of the glare, a fat man wielding a big jam box that played Tejano rock.

Youngsters had taken over one stretch. These tan, slim bodies drew some resentment from me at the way they took it for granted, time and opportunity, their entitlement. A Frisbee glided slow over their heads, and it seemed that for some people the world was forever noon, and I heard their voices and laughs and watched them chase one another like pups. I couldn't imagine Rocky out there. A lot of things never get to become what they should.

Before returning to the motel I stopped at an Ace Hardware and bought a box of double-extra-strength Steel Sak trash bags and thirty feet of half-inch rope.

I ducked inside the office at Emerald Shores, and now Dehra and Nancy sat at a coffee table playing a board game with Tiffany, who looked clean and fresh in a little yellow linen dress. She slapped her hands together at the fall of the dice, looked up, and waved at me.

Nancy raised her eyebrows and I could only shake my head. She walked over.

"You're right," I said. "She don't work there. Never has. I don't know. I cruised around a while but didn't see anything."

"Jesus, Mary, and Joseph." She stuck her hands to her hips. "So, what?"

"How long do they have on the room? I forget what I've paid."

"Y'all are good till the day after tomorrow, I believe."

"I bet she comes back by then."

"Oh, really?"

"I bet she knows just when the rooms stop being theirs. She's going to come back for that little one. If she doesn't, I'll start checking other motels."

"You're just assuming she's all right? Just figure nothing happened to her?"

"She hasn't been gone long enough to think that way." I wasn't letting myself ponder those lines, yet.

Nancy peeked back inside the office. The last of the sun was blocked by buildings, turning the air into a gloomy scarlet haze. We could see Tiffany through the glass, enjoying herself.

"What's the matter with her, then? Having a little one like this. What's wrong with her?"

"I can't really say. You know how it is. Some people. Something happens to them. Usually when they're young. And they never get any better."

"But some do."

"I guess. You tend to meet more of the other kind, though."

She nodded and tapped her foot, eyed a Big Gulp cup someone had left in the parking lot. It rolled back and forth. I bent my head. "Listen. That little girl. If something . . . I don't know. You all would take care of her. Wouldn't you?"

She arched her head back as though mildly insulted. "What?"

Tray's motorcycle caught my eye. Without realizing it, night had come down, and we stood in sudden, deepening blues. "What time is it?"

"Quarter till eight. What were you just saying?"

"Nothing. I have to meet somebody."

"So we have the baby again?"

"I can take her with me, I suppose. But I don't have any more right to her than you." I handed her forty dollars. "There. For dinner. Or entertainment. If Rocky doesn't come back by tomorrow, we'll work something out."

She didn't hesitate to take the money, folded it and slipped the paper into the front pocket of her denims. "She's not always happy, you know. That little one."

"What?"

"Tiffany. She's not always laughing and smiling. Sometimes she gets angry. Real angry. Throws her food and cries about it. She starts asking for the other one, and she gets angry. She's jumpy if you move too fast. I know I already told you."

I didn't really know what I could say about that. I just nodded.

Killer Tray skulked beside a pay phone at the Circle K, shoulders hunched like he was braced against a bitter wind. He waved at me when he saw the truck and jogged over. I'd tossed the rope and garbage bags in the bed.

He opened the door.

"All right," I said.

"You want to see it?"

"Let's just go," I sighed. He directed me toward Broadway and said there was no hurry.

"Basically everything's kept in a storage room. There's a small cloakroom there too, where they keep some lead vests and things, but behind *that*, inside, is like a shaft that used to lead to the roof or something. The panel's bolted shut, but there's a crawl space between floors. The maid'll get me in there, when they're closing. Chill till around one, and I get down, rewire that alarm. We need a van, too. I need you to take care of that. You bring it around back, we load the stuff—twenty minutes, tops. We take it to Houston. And I've done all the hard work."

"What's the address?"

"It's 4515 Broadway."

"Who's your inside again?"

"This maid, man. I used to run with her brother."

"There alleys on the other side? Somewhere we could scope it from?"

"Yeah. Sure. Turn here."

He bounced his knees and tapped his thighs, chewed his bottom lip. I had worked out all kinds of variations of dialog between us, potential scenarios. But even if the score went smooth and we both walked with full pockets, that would just encourage him. No matter what he said about his word, it's a simple fact of the living world that you can't trust a junkie. He'd always have what he knew over the two girls.

I tried not to think about it, because he was like the girl in the motel room in Amarillo: he would never catch a break. It could only go bad.

"Where was your group home?" I asked.

"Huh? Oh. Jasper."

"They ever make you all pick cotton there?"

"Uh. No."

"They did mine. Had us all out there, every August till October. Called the Social Supplement Program."

"Huh."

"You ever have any fosters?"

"Uh, yeah," he said. "Once, when I's eight. They were all right. Then they had to move. Couldn't take me. Something about his job." He pointed to the windshield. "Here we are."

"I'm going to park on the other block. We'll come up through the alley."

"Sure. Okay."

*   *   *

We walked through the alley and stayed in its shadows. A Dumpster, windswept papers. No windows above us. He pointed out the clinic. "I don't know," I said. "Looks pretty open."

"It's not, though, not around back. There's another alley running along there. They got their own loading place in the back."

"I don't know," I said, and let him walk ahead of me. I pulled out the heavy work gloves I'd stuffed in my back pocket, held my breath while I slipped them on. There were plenty ways I could have done it, but he was thin as a kitten and this would work. I was quiet.

When he turned around he jumped back because I'd gotten real close, but it was too late. I caught him around the throat. His eyes filled with a terrible understanding and then they swelled like blood blisters, and I said, *"Shhhh."* That face they always show me—*Wait. Wait.*

He struggled, but I had a good eight inches of reach on him. His face went purple, capillaries swelled and burst under his skin, and he tried for that little knife but it clattered to the ground right when I pressed with my thumbs and felt his hyoid snap. His eyes flittered and rolled backward. The air rattled out his body with a last gurgle, and I smelled his bowels. His tongue slumped out like a fat, exhausted slug.

Setting him down I had the urge to offer an explanation, to convince him it was only because of the girls. That wouldn't have made it go any easier for him, though.

I checked both ends of the alley, where the streetlight cut into the dark, and I pulled my truck up so that the door was flush with the alley. I threw him in the passenger side, propped his body against the heavy tinting of the window.

I'd planned to get out on a feeder road where it was dark, wrap him up in the tarp and tuck it behind the cab, in the bed of the truck. But driving out of town, he seemed to look natural that way, against the door, as if only passed out, and though the cab smelled with his dying shit there was an intimacy persisting between us.

I felt a mutual recognition. Like he knew something about the big empty fields, the one-room apartments, coffee made on a hot plate, the voice that calls *lights out*. And for my part I was the only one who understood the terror of where he found himself at the end of everything, in that alley with me.

I drove him out of town like that, slumped against the door. My drunken friend. My last buddy. My weak and reckless younger self.

La Porte was about thirty miles outside Galveston, and a marsh there fed into Galveston Bay. I had made a couple trips here before, working for Sam Gino. Long time ago. It was the same as I remembered. A backwater called Marais du Chien, a big, black, tangled mess of sinkholes and sloughs that ran in circles, and every part of it looked alike, a maze of cypress and pine and willow crawling with alligators and snakes, ancient garfish the size of canoes. An obsolete irrigation road led to an isolated bend and a patch of forest that dropped into marsh, and these things were still there, only more overgrown, the giant cane and snarled vines and high trees overlaid by a cover of kudzu that made it all seem like a single entity, a prehistoric creature whose leafy silhouette crested along the brighter hem of night.

I kept my lights off on the irrigation road and parked between some pines near the bend. I tore a hole in one of the garbage bags and wore it like a barber's apron, then dumped his body out the truck. I took his keys and wallet, stripped his shirt and pants, and then I cut the cooling flesh under his arms, where the blood was listless and thick.

I was going to slip a few bags over him and use the rope to truss him up, but I heard things splashing and rippling the water, and looking out in the blackness I could almost see the gator push itself into the marsh with a swipe of its tail, heard it break the surface with a soft *plop*. Wings flapped somewhere.

I hoisted him up the rise at the bend. He was light, even as deadweight. I dumped him over my shoulder and he splashed down into the dark. I listened, heard the low rustle and watery sound as things moved to investigate. Then I tossed his clothes into a garbage bag, tied it off, and slung it into the marsh. The water below started churning and splashing.

On the way out of La Porte I dumped his wallet in the trash can outside a McDonald's, and then I stopped at the first store and bought a pint of Jim Beam, which was horrible but all they had.

Rocky still wasn't at the motel, and the lights in the sisters' room were off. I let myself into Killer Tray's room. He didn't have much, but I took what clothes were there and his books and dumped them all in a garbage bag, made sure the coast was clear, and hauled them out to a Dumpster the next block over.

Then I went to my room and showered, tossed my clothes, and sat in the dark facing the window. I sipped from a new, better bottle of whiskey, and smoked cigarettes, watching outside with my knees bouncing and fists clenching.

Sometime around one a long, dark-colored Cadillac floated into the lot, its squared front cutting the blackness with its lights. Not the kind of vehicle you'd expect to wash up here. The windows were tinted and the engine was soft, though you could hear its quiet power humming.

Rocky stepped out the passenger side. She wobbled a little on high heels, and it looked like a new dress she was wearing, something like the hide of a zebra, and it hugged her tightly. She shut the door and kind of staggered backward, as if drunk, and as the car pulled away it caught her squinting in the headlights, and I saw her pause and draw a hand flat against her mouth when she noticed my truck.

When I first opened the door her face wore this smug, dazed expression, but as I marched closer it faded and she became scared, managed to say "*Roy*" in a high, crackling voice.

I didn't break stride but clamped her wrist and pulled her along back to my room.

I threw her inside. She fell on her knees and hit the mattress with her head, a bit dramatically, and I kicked the door shut. Pulled the curtain.

"Roy, *wait*." She inched back on the ground. "Wait." The dress hiked up her legs and one of its straps fell from her shoulder, and I could see a mottling of gray bruise around her upper thigh.

"You shouldn't wear mascara," I said. "You don't know how. You look ridiculous."

She tried to say something as I pulled off my belt, but when she met my glare her voice left her, and her eyes widened on the belt buckle. She had thought it would go one way, that she'd be able to talk and call me names and squirm out of it. "*I thought you were gone!*" she said.

I tugged her up by her hair and held her so she had to stand on her toes to keep her scalp, and tears spilled down the steep slopes of her cheeks.

I just stared at her that way. Her nose was swollen red and her shocked eyes blinked behind a wet glaze, the whites ruptured with red. Probably still high. Her chest heaved.

I slapped her face with my palm and she fell across the bed.

She yelped, "That guy, Tray, he told me you *knew*. He showed me that newspaper!"

"My life," I said. "That little girl's life. You told him about us?"

"What—no—"

I folded the belt and snapped it between my hands.

"Roy, Roy." She fumbled her words, weeping, holding her hands up. "That Tray guy'd been asking about you. He asked me about you first time I met him, that morning we were all out there. I told him you were a tough dude, our uncle, and, like, dangerous. That's it. *I thought you left.* He bought me some beer. All I told him. He showed me the, the—*news-paper—*"

"All that talk about being straight. It don't occur to you to tell me you're a murderer?"

She just shook her head, stared at the floor. "You don't. He—*he—*"

"You made me an accessory. That little girl."

She shook her head.

"And you start whoring the minute I step out."

"*Step out?* I thought you were *gone*. You didn't say anything. Just ran off. Then that Tray guy offered me a beer, told me you took your bags. I had to get some money, man. What'd you expect me to do? What do you care?" She seemed too stunned to stand, and her head lolled on her neck, her words slurred.

"Where'd you get the bruises?"

She pulled her skirt down and shrugged, curled her legs up.

"Same place you got the dress?"

She moaned a long, stuttering sound, like she couldn't catch a breath, mashed her face against her knees, breathing in spasms.

"My God, I'm a stupid son of a bitch." I crouched next to her and let the heavy buckle sway in front her eyes. "It wouldn't matter except you got that little girl with you. You took her out her house and now you got her in *this*. And me. Happens you get busted selling your little ass? What about that? I mean, shit, you realize that's illegal, right? Let's forget the whole issue of dignity and safety and shit—but what the *fuck* are you *doing*?"

I grabbed her by the chin, hard, and tilted her face up. Her nostrils flared and her gaze, paralyzed, had a rabid fervor to it that looked to me like actual madness, barely constrained.

"That woman around the way? *Pick up your head.* Look at me. That woman around the way. She's about to call the cops on you. About to call social services on Tiffany. Going to tell them a whore abandoned her daughter here. You know where that leaves Tiffany? You know what foster care's like? Are you listening? Look at me. You don't have time to cry for yourself, you goddamned trash."

She turned her face away again, shook her head. She said *no* over and over. "I'm sorry, I'm sorry, *I'm sorry!*"

"Cancel that. I don't care. You're going to blow everything for yourself, and you want to pretend you're too dumb to know it."

I kept hateful eyes on her until she stopped heaving. I lifted her up by her arms.

"Talk to me *now*. Tell me what you think you're doing."

"I didn't mean. I mean, I lost track of time."

"With *Lance*? What was that? What about what happened in New Orleans? What about your friend in the bedroom?"

She hissed at me. "What am I— *How was I gonna take care of her? Huh?* We need *money*, Roy! *You left!*" She wiped her nose and straightened her dress. "You're not staying around. I know that. So what was I gonna do? *What do you even care?* What was I gonna do?"

"There's a few hundred answers to that question before you get to whoring, I think. Who was that? In the Caddy?"

"A man. Just. I met him the other night. He was in town a few days and wanted company. He paid good. I can buy up another week here, get food. Some more clothes."

"Look at yourself."

"You think I care?"

"No. I don't rightly know what you care about. I can't imagine. Look at you. You're all coked out."

"No. I-I didn't—" But then she fell to that hard crying again and made like she was incapable of speech. She curled against the bed and put her head in her hands.

"Dammit. It could have been fine, Rocky."

"Where'd you go? *Where'd you go?*"

"Like this is my fault. I got no reason to stay around you, anymore. You understand?"

"Whatever."

I wrapped the belt around my hand and stood over her. The single lamp drew the room's shadows out long and spiny and fell over her face in ghoulish markings. Salt air and the remnants of her sex, musky, damp. The leather creaked around my knuckles. I didn't want to, but it's like beating a dog you love.

It's important to teach it; it's just a shame this is how the stupid animal learns.

But like a double-barreled impact one of those coughing fits struck me, and the weights slammed into my chest. I doubled and spat, savage hacking, flecked with blood.

Stars burst in my eyes, my head swam. I couldn't catch my breath and dropped to my knees. The pain was suffocating, each bark like getting struck in the chest by a sledgehammer. My ribs ached, bruised insides, flashes of light dancing in my vision, and I could picture old Mr. Death marching through my soft tissues, each cough a swat of his cane.

"Roy?" She'd crept closer. "Roy? Come on, man. Are you—should I call?"

I reached out to stop her. Grabbing her hand and squeezing it too hard, holding it like an anchor as I coughed—roars, scraping, parched sounds—but she didn't let go. She held mine with both of hers and squeezed back until I'd stopped, and she kept holding it afterward.

Once it passed I needed some time to gather myself, and when I did my face was wet with tears and snot. I looked at her and I could tell she saw the fear on me.

I wiped my mouth, but there was no blood.

"What'll it take?" I wheezed. I sounded like an old man, someone who'd gargled Drano. "What'll it take? What?"

"Don't. Just don't leave us, man. I *can't*—" She wiped at her face and clutched my hand harder, then let go.

"Christ."

She stroked her palm with the fingers of the other hand, and watched me nervously. "Shouldn't you see a doctor?"

"You need a weatherman to tell you it's raining?"

"But you're sick. Okay? I know you don't want me reminding you. But you're not doing anything about it. You're just drinking. Smoking."

"The way I'm sick. It's not something you get better from."

"Roy . . ." Her face twisted up, slowly, like a child who begins to realize the extent of some bad news. "Back in Orange. I, I-I—" Her stuttering got real bad then, and she brought both hands to her mouth.

"Settle down. You're okay. Nobody's going to connect that with you. I got rid of the gun."

She looked at her lap and started crying, but a different, more sorrowful sort.

"Hey. It's over and done. It was done. This won't come back to you. The only person you need to square it with is yourself."

"I'm so—" She shook her head. "You don't. He used to say, to tell me, *it was my fault*—" Embarrassed grief shuddered over her face, and she seemed like a little girl again, and I could feel how deeply she hated herself.

"I don't doubt he deserved it. Understand? I have *no doubt*. If you told me why, I'd probably have done it myself. It doesn't matter. It's done. You got to forget it."

I stood and helped her up, and when I put my hand on her shoulder she set her head against my chest and cried there.

"That's how it is with these things. You don't have to feel it. You can say what you feel and what you don't. Hold back what you want. If something doesn't work, let it go."

She clutched her arms around me, such nimble strength in them.

"Do you believe in hell, Roy?"

"No," I said. "Or not anywhere but on Earth."

"I have to get Tiffany. Should—"

"I'm going to square it with Nancy. The only reason nobody got called was they all love Tiff so much."

"I know. They do. That's what I thought, Roy, when—I mean, I could see them ladies and see they wouldn't let nothing bad happen to her, or—"

"You can't do that."

"No. I know."

Her knees wobbled and I sat her on the chair. She still needed talking down. I said, "So tell me about him."

"I don't want to." She shook her head.

I thought a moment. "She's not your sister, is she?"

She shot a shocked look at me, then bowed her head again and started crying.

"Okay," I said. "That's all right."

"And I *left* her. I left her behind."

I had no response, just let her sit and steady her breathing. I rubbed my chest and waited for her.

When she spoke her voice was soft, but directed with a new sobriety. "What happened was I got sick. She wasn't around, Mom. Sometimes she left town to work a convention or something, just a couple days, like. But she wasn't around. I'd gotten a flu or something from spending the night under this trestle bridge. That's another story. But when I was home I got fevered and had to stay in bed. It was just me and Gary and so he moved the TV in my room for me, and I remember thinking that was nice of him. We didn't have no medicine around, and he was drinking from a bottle. He said it was good for when you were sick. That his mom'd give him and his brothers a little whiskey to fight off a cold. And so he sat in there with me watching TV, and every now and then he'd offer me a shot in a little Dixie cup. I remember it was a Dixie cup. And after a while I was feeling better, like, happier, and I didn't care that I was sick. And he was telling me jokes and we'd laugh at what was on the TV. The lights were real low, just a couple candles and the TV, and he was sitting beside me in bed, which I didn't feel like minding because I was getting so happy. He was so fat, though, the bed sunk so it kind of rolled me toward him while I was drifting off like. Then, I don't know, it was late—I like woke up, except I must have already been awake. I don't really know how it happened. But I woke up and it was happening. He was on top of me." She shook her head, confounded, as if it were somebody else's story. "He was so fat. Like I couldn't breathe. He had like pimples on his shoulders, big red clusters, and he smelled like crawfish, like mud."

I thought about things you can't survive, even if they don't kill you.

She went on, "Anyway, when Mom gets back. I don't know. I think he told her or something. Told her it was my fault or something. But she was different to me, toward me. I felt like screaming every time I saw him. I didn't know what things were. I didn't understand what was happening. I started getting big and Mom just left. Then Gary was saying how it would be a good thing. He could get benefits from the state." She put her head in her hand. "I started getting big and I couldn't get out the house. He only took me to the hospital at the end."

I leaned toward her. "Go to your room. Take a bath or something. Relax, put it out your mind, *come down*. Get your mind right. This, what you were doing, that's over."

"What're you . . . ?"

"I'm staying in my room. I had a long night, too. In the morning I'll talk to Nancy. I'll have thought of something by then. We can't stay here anymore. We have to leave."

"Okay. Okay. I'm sorry."

"Leave it."

"I'm sorry I made you listen to all that stuff."

I opened the door for her, and she walked out, but paused a second, seeing Tray's motorcycle still outside his room. She looked over her shoulder at me and didn't say anything. I stood in the doorway and watched her step to her room, and she turned back one more time to look at me, as if I might have disappeared, then closed her door.

I spent some time in those early morning hours trying to think my way through to the next right thing. I wanted those girls to have some money. At the center of Rocky was a learned fear of what it really meant to have no means.

Maybe she'd keep on doing the things she did regardless. I wasn't sure that mattered.

I scratched at my chest, and it was tender and sore inside from the violence of my coughs.

My disease had made haste of things. I believe if I'd had a life to live I might have stuck around those girls, tried to make it work for them awhile. But I just wasn't going to last that long.

I watched my smoke break against the curling wallpaper, and as the level in the bottle sank and my thoughts became intuitive, manic, a plan gradually formed.

I dug out the folder from Sienkiewicz's house.

squared things with Nancy and she seemed at least temporarily satisfied about Tiffany's welfare and maintenance. I told her we'd be leaving. I started to walk away and she said, "You seen Mr. Jones around anywhere?"

I stopped, shook my head. "Saw him yesterday, in the afternoon for a little bit. To ask about Rocky." I faced his room. "His bike's still here."

She didn't comment.

"Did he owe for the room?"

"No. He actually had a couple days left."

I didn't say anything else and walked to the girls' room. Rocky sat behind Tiffany, stroking her hair on the bed while they watched television, a talk show. I said, "You need to stay with your sister today. Be good. I'm coming back."

She seemed chastened and washed out, shoulders slumped, and she spoke softly without turning to me. "What're you doing?"

"I'm working on something. I'll be back later. It's something for you all."

"Okay." She studied Tiffany's hair, her face passive and careless. Her fingers moved automatically, coglike.

I made sure they had a little money, and I drove to San Marcos to start a bank account with First National.

I'd restudied the papers in the folder. Manifests, shipping arrivals and departures, with handwritten notes that recorded the vanishing of certain containers which were circled red and doubly referenced in an accounting notebook that described payments and shipping losses in a surprisingly plain style of recording, no codes to cipher or floating figures between margins. The name Ptitko was fairly abundant. I suppose Frank Sienkiewicz thought this would be like insurance for him, something to keep him safe.

Pretty stupid, actually. Maybe he was trying to make a deal with prosecutors and there was a tip-off. Maybe he threatened Stan with it. I don't know.

First National had branches all over the place, including New Orleans, and I could call on a phone from anywhere and get an account balance by punching in a few numbers.

All you needed back then was a driver's license and secondary form of ID. I attached the account to the mailing address on my license, somewhere in Alexandria.

This took most of the day, and when I returned in the late evening I looked in on the girls. Rocky had taken to bed. She lay staring at the ceiling while the television droned and Tiffany amused herself with a stuffed bear the old women had bought for her.

"Hey. You all right?"

She blinked at the ceiling, its map of gray-brown water stains.

"You feeling sick?"

"No."

"Well. What's going on?"

She spoke drily and with a slackened mouth, but her eyes flinched a little and seemed to concentrate, as if she watched a movie playing out on the blotched plaster above. "I'm just resting. I'm just tired, Roy."

The girl arched her head back to watch us, and the bear hung limp in her hands, which were wrapped around its neck as if she'd choked it.

"You're not sick?" I asked.

"No. I'm not. Really."

Tiffany's eyes went back and forth between us, searching for clues, and a sliver of fear pulsed across my back. I wondered for maybe the dozenth time what might lie ahead for her, and I thought of the girl at the truck stop in Amarillo.

Rocky spoke again. "I'm just resting up, Roy. I'm just coming down and getting my head straight. Don't worry. I'll be fine." Her pupils moved like they were following a hive of motion. "A good night's sleep, I'll be fine."

"I'm leaving again for a bit. Just a few hours, is all. I shouldn't have to leave again. So I don't want you to worry. Watch your sister and I'll be back late tonight. That's thirty bucks. Get a pizza or something."

"Okay."

Tiffany twisted the toy back and forth in her hands, its arms flapping.

"I thought maybe we could go out tomorrow," I said, and it sounded a little stupid, but I felt like I needed to leave her with something, a promise of some kind to see her through the night. "Maybe just the two of us. Dinner. Something like that."

"Sure. That sounds nice, Roy."

"All right. Well, see you, girls."

"What're you going to do, really?"

"Make a phone call."

The air outside was black and starless, and rain felt certain in the dense atmosphere. One of the truck's headlights was fad-ing on me, and ahead the left-side beam flickered and dimmed, a drizzle blinking on and off. If they had a way of finding out the area code or something, I thought it best to make the call away from the city. I drove a couple hours into Louisiana, up to Leesville. Just in case.

The pay phone leaned outside an abandoned gas station, the soft earth sunken on one side. The fuel prices on the sta-tion's signs were all blank, and the windows of the office next to the garage were covered in garbage bags that had been cut and stretched over. I thought of the bags I'd bought for Tray, and my hands started shaking. At the pay phone I took a couple nips from a J&B pint, stood in the booth, and smoked a cigarette. The thick forests that bordered the old highway screamed with insects, and the concrete lot fractured where weeds had sprung up like stiff hair, chalk yellow under the streetlight that hunched over the phone booth like a protective mother. Outside its glow the trees rattled in the wind.

When my cigarette was finished I smoked another one. Then I held the receiver in my hand, dropped my dimes, and dialed.

I had to roundabout with the bartender, George, and I almost asked him how his ear was doing.

"Tell him it's Roy," I said.

A couple long minutes passed while I waited for him to come on the line, and I listened to the insects and watched moths and mosquitoes hover and try to rise in the jaundiced light. Before he spoke I heard a click, a slight increase in static, but I knew he had this thing attached to his office line that kept anyone from listening to his calls.

"This must only be someone fucking with me," said the voice on the other end. It was deep and scratchy as a bullfrog's, stilted too, bent around his New Orleans accent, and he always enunciated precisely. "This really you?"

"It's really me," I said, and I heard him inhale a cigarette, could hear the burning tobacco crackle. I thought of Carmen smiling over her shoulder at him. I felt exposed in the streetlight, alone with the empty road, the shrieking darkness.

He said, "Some piece of work. I mean, that was impressive."

"I didn't have any choice about that."

"No. I can see that. We cleaned it up. Damn, though. I wondered if we'd hear from you, you know?"

"Surprise, surprise." I heard his cigarette pop and snap softly and I could picture his round, frowning face, the contempt in that calculating, beady stare and the smoke drifting out his nostrils.

"You coming back around here?" he asked.

"I wouldn't imagine."

"Yeah. Figured."

"Why, though? I don't get it."

"Why what?" he said.

"Why'd you do for us like that, Stan? I mean *for what?*"

"You got it wrong, Big Country. This wasn't us. It was Armenians. They had their own thing with the guy. Their business. You guys all just showed up at the same time. Bad luck for us. They didn't mean to get into it with you. They were just there for him."

"Really?"

"Absolutely. Bad luck. But hey, bad luck for them, right?"

"You're straight?"

"Word of honor."

I studied my reflection in the smudged, cracked glass of the booth. I didn't look like myself. I'd lost about eight pounds in the last week, and all my hair was gone. "Except," I said, "you told us not to bring any guns. Remember that?"

He didn't say anything. I think he put out his cigarette.

"Stan?"

"Ah. All right. You got me."

"You got that much of a problem with anybody who's laid pipe to her, you're gonna have a few hundred bodies to put down."

"Watch that shit, Big Country."

"To do us like that, over what. *Her?* It's grotesque."

"Ah. That's not really it, though. You. Angelo. You aren't exactly key to the enterprise, you know? The thing was: Why not do it? Like smashing a spider. Three birds, one stone. You two go down for Sienkiewicz. You know? Why *not* do it? The why is because I fucking say so. The why is *I decide.*"

"Your mind's a pit of snakes."

"You understand."

I swallowed hard and took a deep breath. I focused on the wavering leaves that outlined the edge of the darkness.

"So," I said. "I have something."

"So."

"Cargo manifests. Records. A ledger that explains transactions real clearly. Your name everywhere. A really long and really detailed letter explaining operations. All in the dude's handwriting. I guess this is what the supersoldiers wanted."

I heard something smash on the other side of the line.

"*Shit-eyes,*" he said. "On *my eyes*—"

"On *your* eyes, then. You called it down, you Polack greaseball *motherfucker*. This is what they were there for, right? This thing Sienkiewicz put together."

Smoldering static on the line. The bugs filled the lamp's cone of light like flakes in a snowglobe. Movement—shadows fell from the trees to the south. The road lit up as headlights exploded. An engine's growl, and my heart skipped as a van cruised past, blinding me for an instant and washing me in gasoline fumes, yanking my shadow tall across the lot.

"Where you calling from?" Stan asked.

"Doesn't matter."

"What do you want?"

"Seventy-five K. Deposited."

"Heh."

"It's a bargain."

"I think it's a bit much."

"Copies go out. *Times-Picayune.* Baton Rouge. Something national. The original to the feds. 'Ptitko,' it says. Right here. Nearly every page. 'Ptitko.'"

"Still."

"Get a pen, because I'm about to hang up."

"See, though? What assurances do I have?"

"You can be assured if anything happens to me it'll go out anyway."

"I don't want to be hearing about this the rest of my life. I don't want you calling again when you blow through the cash."

"I guess you'll have to figure that my word is better than yours. As long as I stay breathing, it stays safe. I read about the guy they have in charge, the fed attorney, Whitcomb. I read in the paper he's real fired up about Sienkiewicz going missing." He didn't respond to that. "This buys me out. I'm done. You got a pen?"

"Wait."

"No." I read him the account number with First National. I said to make the deposit by four the next day or I was going to the post office. Then I hung up.

My hands had started shaking again and my knees weakened, wobbled. I took a hard pull off the J&B. I stepped out the booth and threw up. Gnats and mosquitoes lighted on the bile and circled my head like a crown.

The one dimming headlight held my vision on the drive back, and I pulled from the bottle and kept the radio off. My foot kept slipping off the gas pedal.

On the island scattered fires trembled on the beaches. The wind was loud off the water. But for the low-lit sign and a desk lamp in the office, the motel was dark. Lance's grill stood outside his door again.

I peeked through the break in the curtains of the girls' room and the faint blue glow of the television undulated over them. Rocky was curled, bunching the covers, and Tiffany lay next to her, her arms and legs kicked loose and splayed in a big T-shirt. I had the same fearful sense I had as a boy, when my stomach would hurt and my back would become stiff, and I would want to wander alone in the fields for days like a sick dog.

The next day I mentioned to the two old ladies that we'd be leaving. It was another humid white day, salty and wet. We were going to let Tiffany go to the beach a last time and they asked if they could come with us. The walk was slow with them, and I lugged their two aluminum lawn chairs and Rocky carried a big canvas bag with everyone's towels and things. She was more responsive today, and that morning she'd asked me where we were going on our big date. I'd forgotten suggesting that.

Still, there was a bored sadness to her. And a resignation I'd seen on faces my whole life—people giving up, crossing over to that place without struggle—and I wanted to alter that.

The women wore their dark polyester-suit clothes, even to the beach, and they trundled up the sand with Tiffany, their stockings thick and brown and even then their varicose veins were visible in dark squiggles. The breeze rippled my big Hawaiian shirt as I set up their chairs. They lowered themselves real careful under wide-brimmed hats and sun-shades they'd slipped over their regular eyeglasses. Rocky seemed shy around the women as she stripped to her suit and they glanced over her. I sat on the sand next to the sisters for a bit, and we all watched Rocky lead Tiffany out to the waves.

I could make out from here the bruising on her thigh, but she still looked good, that lean body and rosy pale skin, the lithe muscle and truly first-rate butt. Part of Rocky was this great beauty she wouldn't let into the light yet, because it had never found its proper place. I believe that.

She guided Tiffany into the water, the little girl still shocked and cringing at the waves, then bursting with laughter when they broke over her. It made Rocky laugh too, and she'd lifted the girl up and let the waves sweep over her legs, and we could hear their laughter popping and blending with the hiss of the water.

Other people were out there and more appearing. Families, kids and teenagers, dark brown guys with sun-bleached hair who watched Rocky as they passed.

The ladies clucked and giggled over Tiffany as her squeals carried up the beach. Sweat beaded the women's jowls and they dabbed at it with a shared handkerchief.

Dehra said, "She's such a good spirit. Such warmth."

"Yes," her sister said. "Such a good disposition."

"I, uh, appreciate how much you all have taken to the little one," I said.

"She's very special."

"She is."

"I think so, too," I said. I waited a bit and added, "It might be the case that they end up staying here awhile, after I leave."

Their faces admitted just the barest hint of confusion under the big hats and shades.

"They need people to be nice to them. That little girl needs people looking out for her, if they end up sticking around."

"What do you mean?" Dehra asked.

"I mean, if I wasn't around. If the little one needed something."

"Oh." They glanced at each other.

"I know you all would watch out for her."

"Well, you know, we've never really—"

"It's all right," I said, waving my hand. I stood up then and walked out to the beach. The sand pulled at my feet and made my legs heavy.

At the water they were smiling at me, and Tiffany thrust her arms up and shook her hands for me to lift her. I waded into the warmth and grasped her beneath the arms, and she shouted when I tossed her in the air, kicking her legs and screeching so she could make the most of the escape from gravity. Splashing, the sting of salt.

Rocky's dimples looked sincere for a second, and she smoothed the wet hair across her scalp. Light sparkled out the water on her skin and in her eyes, in her teeth, but I kept catching sight of those small gray clouds on her thigh. She said, "You decided where you're wining and dining me?"

I turned around and saw up the beach. One of the two women was lowering a little camera they'd brought. Then they both just sat, frozen in their dark clothes, nunlike, their faces blank and shaded. Something about the doubling of the figures seemed conspiratorial. I thought about that bank account.

The office was crowded with three bouquets of new flowers, gifts from Lance, I supposed. I was going to pay Nancy to watch Tiffany that night, but the ladies asked to have her, which surprised me because of their reluctance when I mentioned it on the beach. I went to the supermarket and rented some cartoons for them to watch.

Around four thirty I phoned First National, and the money wasn't there, only the fifty bucks I'd used to start the account.

I stopped at a half booth next to a bodega where wetbacks patted their stomachs and drank beer from paper bag coolies on the sidewalk. It didn't matter where I called from. I was gone the next morning.

"The *fuck?*" I said into the phone.

"I had to make some transfers, but they don't go through till tomorrow. I wanted to tell you but you didn't leave me no number."

"The packages are bundled and stamped, addresses on."

"Cut the drama shit, please. You want it, it'll be there tomorrow. That's all I can tell you."

I hung up. The Mexes eyed me as I bought a pint in the bodega and took a quick hit on the sidewalk. They met my eyes, which isn't ordinary, and their silent, unsympathetic stares seemed to carry judgment on me, like the gaze of that girl in Amarillo, and they kept watching as I climbed back into the truck.

I came closest to making a run for it then.

Rocky had done some shopping, I guess. She wore a nice little outfit, a long light skirt with cornflowers on it and a sleeveless top with a high neckline, and the discretion it afforded seemed meant to please me, but I didn't want to think about how she'd gotten the money for it.

She looked excited, like this was enough of a normal thing to prod her back to that state of endurance where she strove to be earnest and tell the truth. She'd even gotten the mascara right, a light, fine brushing that made dark feathers of her lashes, and I thought these might be the eyes of the woman she would one day become.

Lance had set up the VCR in the sisters' room, and I watched them lead Tiffany away as she hopped and studied the two videos I'd rented.

On the way out we passed the office and Lance was standing in front of the desk. He peeped at us, then returned to making some kind of fervent plea to Nancy, who had her arms folded, and also glanced our way.

"Where'd you like?" I said. "Downtown? One of those nice places?"

She thought and shook her head. "Somewhere like that place we first drank at. When we just met, you know? In Lake Charles. That was kind of cool. A country bar or something."

"I'm pretty sure we can find one of those."

The end of the sun washed over us, and she talked about how much she liked the ocean here, and the music on the radio. She was putting me in a good mood, and I felt a little ridiculous for it, to feel some illusion of freedom in that sea air through the windows, the bonfires and the waves. I tried talking about what sorts of things she might see herself doing one day, but she kept turning the subject back to the weather, the ocean.

I took us west a ways to Angleton, where there was no short-age of roadside taverns. We decided on a larger one called Long-horn's, a good-looking place built of long cypress logs, just a little too upscale for people looking to fight, an oyster-shell lot and several trucks parked at odd angles to its front.

Heavily varnished tables arranged around a hardwood dance floor, and a small, raised platform for a DJ and band. A few dim lanterns gave sepia glow to frames of Western films hung on post beams. Rounding one side of the tables, a bar occupied the entire wall, and I bought us a pitcher of Lone Star.

She waited for me with her hands crossed primly on the table, her back straight. I poured and she thanked me, this kind of formality to her that was endearing, like she was trying to make up to me.

A waitress whose nose crinkled when she spoke left us two menus and told me she'd be happy to fetch the beers from now on. Rocky started looking over the food list. It was all burgers and steak, and we asked the waitress to give us a minute.

We drank on the pitcher and talked some.

"A lot of these waitresses, they make good money. They raise kids on it."

She nodded.

"Or if you can answer phones and smile."

"I get it, I get it." She filled up my glass. I lit her a cigarette, and we sat there and didn't say much till the pitcher was nearly gone. People had started coming in, old cowboy couples mostly, women in jeans, men in Stetsons.

"Look," I said. "The other night. I don't want us to have to go through something like that again. You won't make it."

"No." Her eyes immediately took on a wet sheen. "No. Don't worry. I'm—" She shook her head and scowled at her beer, squeezed the mug with both hands. "I don't know what it is. There's something not right with the way I think sometimes. Something like—I'll get an idea. And it's just an *idea*. But I'll believe it. I'll just get an idea and act like it's real. And, I don't— it scares me, man. It makes me scared because of the way I act. Things where I'd normally say, '*What are you doing, girl?*' But I'll *think* I'm right. Like, that's the place where I think the idea is real, and I'm right, and I do crazy things."

Her mouth was unsteady, eyes down to her glass, where she traced a circle around its rim. "Like I just go *off* somewhere."

I nodded. "I know something about that."

She kept scowling, twisted the mug in her hands, her knuckles whitening against it. I did something weird. I reached out and took one of her hands in mine, and I laid them on the table. Her whole hand could fit in my palm and she turned it over, gripped mine back.

"I thought you'd left," she said.

"I didn't. Really."

"I know. Now."

The waitress refilled our pitcher and didn't ask about the menu. The lights went down over the dance floor and George Strait started singing, that rich sober drawl, and people rose to step onto the floor, the old couples out early, men with belt buckles the size of human hearts.

"It can't go on though, Rocky. Whether I'm here or not."

"I know it. I *know*."

"You got that little one now. It's over. Forever."

"I get confused."

We drank on the new pitcher and watched the couples turn slowly and two-step across the floor, and by the fourth or fifth song pale green and purple lights from the stage started gliding over them and the smooth glossy boards like ghostly fish, and the next song was quiet and sad in a prideful sort of way. Women with puffy hair and big asses in tight jeans, love all over their faces. A fog of tobacco smoke lingered above us and held the light.

"I get scared about it," she said. "About Tiff. I worry about what I done. And bringing her, I mean. What I done. Man. *What I've done*."

I leaned over and got her to look up at me.

"The past isn't real."

"What?"

"Tell yourself that. The past isn't real. It's just one of those ideas you get that you think is real. It doesn't exist, baby."

Her brow furrowed and her little mouth hung open, muted.

"Everything starts now. That's it. Right now."

She wiped her eyes and turned to the people on the floor.

I said, "And don't get excited, but I got something going. It could take care of you all awhile."

"What do you mean?"

"Say you had some money. What would you do?"

"How much money?"

"Enough. Rent's paid. Food and bills are paid. For a good while."

Her eyes drifted and she seemed to think, absently traced a fingernail in the condensation ring on the table.

"Okay. I'll tell you what you do. You get yourself to take one of those high school degree tests." She scoffed, and I said, "I'm serious. For real. You hire somebody to help you watch that little girl. And you go to school for something."

"School?"

"That's right."

"But how'd—"

"Say you could afford it. *That* is what you *do*. I just told you. Doesn't matter what you go for. But you learn something. You're quick. Learn to *do* something." I took hold of both her hands. "You do it for yourself or you do it for her, but you do it." She stared at me until most of the fear had left her eyes. "You're strong enough to live the one way, now live the other," I said. "All that starts now."

"Okay, Roy. Okay."

We listened to the song conclude and watched the couples exhaust their orbits. I noticed I still held her hands and let them go, curling my fingers back.

"When do you know about it?"

"What?"

"The money. You know."

"Tomorrow."

"What if it doesn't happen?"

I shrugged and finished my glass. "I think of something else."

Her gaze seemed a little bleary from the beer, and she finished her drink, wiped her mouth. "Did you—?" She let the question die on her tongue.

"What?"

She swallowed hard and folded her fingers together. "Did you do something, to that Tray guy?"

"No." I smiled. "Just scared him probably. Told him to stay away from you and get the hell outta here. He's probably ripping off drugstores in Corpus by now, trying to get himself shot."

"Oh." She watched my face a moment, but there was nothing in it for her to read, and we both looked out at the revolving lights on the empty dance floor. Glen Campbell now.

"Well." Her beer-glazed eyes twinkled, and her smile opened her whole face, like parting shutters onto summer. "You gonna dance with me or what?"

I shook my head, chuckled, and she made a face of mock terror. She led me out to the floor with that same gentle determination as when she'd walk Tiffany to the ocean, and I was drunk enough to not feel totally foolish.

A few people gave us looks from their tables, but they didn't stare long. I towered over her, and had to hunch and watch my feet against hers.

She held herself to me with her face against my sternum, and we rocked back and forth as a few cowboys and ladies revolved around us in the cool gloom with the ghost fish swimming over us all, and her hair smelled like salt water and the sun.

I don't know how many songs played, but we ended up not

eating. We drank some more beer and she told me a couple jokes that were really good, and I remember laughing hard.

She told me stories. She told me about riding around in the backseat of a car when her mother went on this strange date to a group of trailers in the woods. She talked about her school dance team, and how she had to drop out of it when she got pregnant. She told me about leaving school and spending every day, day after day, in that little cabin in the fields.

We danced some more.

It was late when we left, and she walked lightly, bouncing and swaying a little. She kept thanking me. The night was blue at the edges of the lot and shaded darker under the trees where I'd parked.

As we neared the truck, something in its stance struck me as wrong. I fumbled with my keys and noticed the left back tire was totally flat, pancaked, and I looked over the hood at her and said, "Hey—"

Men stood behind her. They'd just appeared. I heard the oyster shells crunch.

Then the pipe struck across my eyes.

Somebody had my arms. I started bucking and the back of my head exploded. Nauseous, skull-cracking pain.

I knew something had broken in me, in my head.

Then I was tasting the dust in my blood, looking at the oyster shells on the ground as they dragged and scraped against my face. I was dripping a lot of blood onto the shells. My arms pulled ahead. My vision had cracked down the middle, and the two sides wouldn't align. I heard muffled screaming.

I heard the van's door slide open, and then they hit me again.

Sharp pains at my shoulders. They were tugging me by my arms and my feet dragged across gravel. They'd taken off my boots. Footsteps crunching, hard breathing. I tried to move my arms but they didn't work. I could see the backs of their knees and their shoes. Stars lined the horizon. I twisted my face up and saw the crusty brown bricks and the sign that said STAN'S PLACE. I screamed.

I couldn't see Rocky. I couldn't hear her, but I was screaming.

They dropped my arms to kick me until I went out again.

I woke with my face on cold concrete, inside tight, dark walls, a small room. I could feel the boys standing around me, in shadows. I wondered who it was, if Lou or Jay was there. Only one of my eyes worked and my vision was doubled in it.

I recognized the storage room. I could see the steel freezer door at the back and the door to the supply room off to the side. I knew there was a hallway out to the right and a set of rooms along it.

I heard Rocky again, just for a second, from somewhere down that hallway—a short, strangled sound.

Somebody nearby laughed at me. Somebody tossed down the folder of papers on the floor by my face. I hacked blood clots onto it.

One of them said, "Stay with us, Big Country. We're waiting on Stan. You gotta have something left for him."

I tried moving but could only sort of wriggle. My hands weren't operational. The pain had layers, and it was deep—you just kept discovering new and greater depths. The men's legs congealed out of the dark, shiny jogging pants and slacks, boots and sneakers surrounding me.

One said, "You supposed to be sick or something, Big Country?"

"You scared the shit out that doctor."

"You scared him so much he lit out. Spent a few days doping in Bay St. Louis."

"Then he comes and sees Stan to get him to make you lay off. So Stan calls his girl at the phone company. And she goes and finds out your number."

That was the first time I remembered calling the doctor.

"Stupid, man. That's really fucking stupid, Big Country. You redneck shit heel."

I thought I heard Rocky's muffled voice raise again, behind the door, furious, gaining in pitch, then choked out, silent.

The shoes closed in on me, and a baseball bat and a long pipe hung beside their knees. I pissed myself. I tried to rise and either the bat or the pipe swung out and cracked my jaw.

I spat teeth. My tongue had ripped. They started in on me again.

The next time I woke up I was tied to a chair and could hardly breathe. My chest burned and my smashed nose gurgled. I'd vomited into my lap, and the concrete under me glistened with blood. I knew this was still the storage room. An air vent dripped in the corner, where just a little light was cast by a mechanic's lamp hung high up there, and it reminded me of the single orange lamp in the foyer of Frank Sienkiewicz's house. It occurred to me that I'd never left that foyer. I was still there and had only dreamed I escaped.

My vision was shoddy out the one eye, but I could see on its periphery all these lumps and strange shapes on my face.

The chair was heavy, a solid hardwood job, and my arms were

cinched so tight my back spasmed in pain from the angle. My chest was tied too tightly to the chair back, my ankles to its legs. It smelled like I'd shit myself. Even with my crushed nose packed with blood, I could still smell it.

I knew they were going to take a long time with me. I'd heard those stories about Stan handling an acetylene torch.

I started crying.

I wasn't thinking about Rocky or her sister. I just didn't want to be hurt anymore. I cried hard, and every time my chest heaved it slid knives into my shoulders and ribs. There was nothing I wouldn't have done to survive. I was going to beg. I'd do anything.

The vent continued dripping in the corner and I could barely make out dim voices behind me, which would be the main bar area, and a steady, subaudible murmur beneath. I realized they were watching TV up there.

Sitting around drinking beer, watching TV, waiting for Stan. I started crying louder.

A door sounded behind me, a soft, hinged squeak, and then I heard it hush shut. I could feel another person here, in back of me, like the air had gone thicker with presence.

I couldn't catch my breath and the tears crawled down my face and stuck to the blood. Quiet footsteps clicked on the concrete. I think I was trying to say *Please*. Or *Wait*.

Wait.

Then a scent or character cohered out of the dark, air like Camel menthols and gin and powder and Charlie perfume. It doesn't seem likely that I could smell that in my condition, but I felt it, the air taking that shape, and I knew who was in the room with me.

She whispered, *Shhhh*. "Be *quiet*. Don't make a sound."

Carmen's shushed voice warm on the back of my neck. My wrists tugged and it killed my shoulders. I whimpered and she hissed, "*Shut up*." The electrical cords binding my wrists fell away, slapped against the floor, left my arms limp at my sides. The rope that bound my torso slipped off.

I could see her then, as she came around to my front. She

kneeled before me and glanced up, those hard, conniving eyes registering fear and even pity, rushed, but still pausing on my face and wincing at it. In that sparse gray light Carmen crouched on the bloody concrete, and my chin sat on my chest as she used a small knife to cut through the tape around my ankles.

She stood up. Her eyes flinched and her mouth curled in a shamed sort of disgust. Her mascara had run and black rivulets stained her cheeks like her eyes had squirted ink. She glanced over her shoulder at the far door and put the knife in my wet hand.

She closed the fingers of my hand around the knife for me. I whimpered, it hurt so badly to move my fingers. She held my hand closed and whispered, "Stand up, Roy. *Stand up.*"

I think I asked about Rocky, because her eyes trembled and she just shook her head. She helped me stand and then let go, and I almost fell over. But my legs weren't too bad. It was everything else.

She said, "*Get out of here.* Run, Roy. Don't look back. *Run* out of here." Her husky speech soaked from tears, her voice almost sounded angry somehow, like I'd wronged her.

I wanted to say something, but my jaw didn't work, and my tongue was so swollen it filled my mouth. Carmen slid away, and I heard the muffled click of her heels on the floor and the door's hinge squealed and opened.

The wall was cold and I leaned against it, my face sticking to the cinder block. My limp hand cradled the knife. My other was useless. The fingers were all crooked.

Stunning, bone-deep aches shot through my feet and shins when I tried to walk. The doorway to the hall seemed a long way off, and little things crackled in me every time I took a step.

I'd blink and be on my knees, see the mechanic's light in the corner, the drips echoing.

Then the tall grasses and the lake.

The stained concrete floor, cold, dark wet.

The cotton fields at night, crickets buzzing.

Spades in junior high. *Fuck you lookin' at, cracker? Kick your peckerwood ass.*

I slumped outside the storage room, crossing the dark hallway, where a red exit sign glowed at the end. A supply closet, a bathroom, another office. The television sounded a laugh track far behind me, and I dragged myself away from it using the bricks in the wall, leaving blood like a slug's trail. I passed the office. That's where Rocky was.

They'd knocked everything off the desk, and she sprawled across it. Her clothes were on the floor, lying on the blotter and pens and papers they'd thrown there. A lamp on top of a filing cabinet cast down a shroud of brass light across her body. Her limp face hung toward the door and her dull grayed eyes met mine, empty, her expression shocked, indicting. A necktie wrapped around her neck. The tie was paisley, I remember.

I left her there.

I threw myself into the door's long handlebar, clanging the hard metal, and then I was on the gravel parking lot, the night both dark and bright, purple and gold, and it all smeared. I stumbled up and a streetlight flashed on the knife in my hand, painted with my blood. I doddered and blundered into a man coming around the corner of the Dumpster, zipping up his fly.

Jay Meires's face twisted when he saw me, and then he snarled, reached for something, and I threw myself on him. I plunged my thumb into one of his eyes and fell with my weight till the eyeball burst, and my thumb kept going farther in. He almost screamed, but it was quick. I put the knife in his other.

I sat on his neck and kept stabbing at his head.

I pulled myself up, still alone, standing over Jay's ruined face.

Bushes. Parked cars. We were behind the bar, and a block ahead, past a vacant lot, a stream of crossing cars broke the night. I started limping as fast as I could for the road. Voices rose behind me.

I was in the field, the dark grass slicing my arms, and they were yelling at me from the bar.

I started dreaming again and when I opened my eye I was standing in the middle of the road. Car lights blazed over me, brakes squealing. Headlamps fractured, blinded me.

I started screaming, waving my hand. A few cars almost hit me and one swatted my elbow with its side mirror, spun me around, and the car screeched to a halt.

White flared in my eyes. People honking. I was crying and screaming. I thought the boys were right behind me.

I yanked open the driver's door and the man inside tried to drive away. I can still see his face, mouth gaping, eyes wide. Somehow I put the knife in him. Pulled his shirt and tossed him out the car.

They found me less than a mile away, smashed into the side of a CPA's office with the steering wheel in my chest.

woke in the bleached, sterile lighting of a hospital, so thirsty I couldn't stand it, and when I tried to open my mouth a shattering pain nearly drove me unconscious. Two policemen were posted outside my door. Gauze patched over my left eye, and later I'd learn that I lost it. My hairline was jagged, my eyebrows ripped, bristled with coarse stitches, my nose fattened and spread like margarine.

Nobody would tell me anything. A couple cops stood by while someone from the D.A.'s office told me about the charges, but I couldn't speak yet or write anything with my mangled hand. My tongue was fat, dry as sandpaper, and its stitches scraped the roof of my mouth. I could feel the bolts in my skull without touching them.

The man I'd stabbed lived. The attorney didn't mention Rocky's body, or Jay Meires. Nobody mentioned Stan Ptitko.

Two weeks later NOPD officers escorted me out of the hospital and to the city jail's infirmary. I told the city's lawyer my story about what happened, about Stan Ptitko and Angelo Medeiras and Frank Sienkiewicz, and Rocky. All of it. The man said I needed to be properly deposed, and that they'd have to wait until I wasn't on so many drugs, painkillers and such, because the defense could play games with that. There was something with the feds, too, like these local guys wanted to keep me away from the feds. An assistant D.A. said they'd get me off the medication for a couple days and take my full statement.

Without the pills, sick, pulsing headaches beat out on me. Another attorney came to visit. The cops must have thought he was my lawyer. They brought me to a visiting area shaped like a railcar, with a counter bisected by an iron mesh grating that cut the room in two. Institutional green walls, that heady, metallic smell of desperation. I sat down and faced through the wire a man in a suit.

His head looked soft and pink like a pencil eraser, with a ring of short dark hair hung around his ears and thick red lips, glasses, all his features blunted and plump. Round nose, round double chin and knoblike ears. His suit made him look slimmer than he was, as did his heavy glasses, and he set a briefcase down on his side of the counter and opened it, but I couldn't see what was inside.

It occurred to me that I recognized him, that he was someone who knew Stan.

"Mr. Cady," he said. "I am speaking to you now as outside counsel for an unnamed party who believes themselves tangentially concerned with your recent felonies. It is my understanding that your speech is extremely limited at this point, so I will proceed from that understanding in order to explicate my reasons for meeting with you."

An expandable gold watchband nestled in the thick hair of his wrist. The shiny surface of his fingernails passed over some papers, closed the briefcase. A crushing, white-light headache was coming on like a freight train.

"My interest in your case is to determine for the sake of my client's representation whether you intend, as part of your own defense, to attempt to indict other persons in your crimes. Ostensibly to lessen the punitive consequences of your actions."

I could only cock my head at him. He spoke with a put-on, overenunciated purr, an old-world Southern accent that rounded off, like all his features.

"In other words, are you planning on making it easy for yourself by pointing the finger at somebody else?"

I nodded: *affirmative.* The screws in my head dug down. A sheriff's deputy stood at the door, facing away from us but alert.

The lawyer nudged his glasses up his nose. "This is what I am here to ascertain, so that my client might have a chance to assemble an effective defense. Now. Naturally that defense would include a body of witnesses to cross-examine in corroborating or disputing your version of events."

I watched him with the bones around my eyes throbbing, and I focused on the metal grating between us, where the paint had chipped and flaked to rust.

"*So*—that witness list would include persons we presume you were most recently acquainted with, correct? Whom you traveled and associated with. This would include one Nancy Covington, owner and operator of the Emerald Shores motel in Galveston, Texas. Correct?" He moved a sheet of paper to the top of his briefcase and appeared to read it. "This would include a young child. Correct? A four-year-old girl, I believe."

The screws in my skull felt like they were twisting deeper and I thought about the metal grating. How completely a man could depend on a thin sheet of iron mesh. The lawyer didn't even know it, or maybe on some level he did, but that screen between us was the most precious and important thing in his life right then. He kept reading.

"The name I have here is a Tiffany Benoit. Currently residing with Nonie and Dehra Elliot, as we speak, at one 540 Briarwood Lane in Round Rock, Texas. Correct? These people. This is the same person. Correct? You were traveling with her. Is that correct?"

Now he stopped at last and we just stared at each other.

That's what the whole visit was about. They'd wanted me to know that they knew about the little girl. Knew where she was.

The lawyer just got up and left me alone shortly after that, even though I hadn't answered any of his questions, and I figured now at least I could get back on the pain meds, because my deposition was blown.

My story changed drastically. Now I told the D.A.'s office that I couldn't remember what had happened.

This wasn't my first arrest or my first trial, and they got after me hard because they were pissed that I'd changed my story.

Thirteen years in Angola.

I just ate it.

The port investigations dropped off.

I didn't figure I'd last much longer anyway, and I didn't want to, because too often when I closed my eyes now I saw Rocky's face, slack and tilted up to the light of the lamp, her body laid as if that desk were an altar.

I was glad I wouldn't have to live with that much longer.

I limped now, from the car wreck, and I wore a patch on my left eye along with a new face, asymmetrical, ridged, my eyebrows misaligned, nose like a piece of spoiled fruit. My fingers never straightened quite right and the knuckles stayed fat and killed me when it rained. The state gave me new teeth. So many were broken that the dentist just pulled whatever was left and made bridges.

A doctor finally looked at me again, and he couldn't say for sure what the spots in my chest were. He wanted to do a bronchoscopy or CT-guided biopsy. He figured it was the same thing as the other doctor. There was a slight chance it might be tuberculosis or sarcoidosis. At best the irregularities were currently benign, but they would almost surely not stay that way. The cysts or carcinomas were in a kind of stasis, as he explained it, and at any time they could turn malignant, metastasize. They needed to do surgery on me. He wanted to slice them out, have a look. Many treatment strategies, he said. They'll move you to a nicer place when you undergo treatment. It was only a matter of time, he said. Unless you're some kind of medical miracle.

I told him no. When he said that the state would pay the costs I told him no again.

For the first couple years I shared a cell with a black man named Charlie Broedus. We got along all right and I wasn't bitter at him when he got released. I kept expecting to die.

After a month inside I went to the library, looking for something to read. I didn't know where to start. A state librarian came in twice a month, and she suggested things. That's how I became friendly with the librarian, Jeanine.

There was no dramatic awakening of personality between us. I think she just liked seeing a convict check out something besides law books.

When I read I got involved in the words and what they were saying so that I didn't measure the passing of time in typical ways. I was surprised to learn that there was this freedom made of nothing but words. Then I felt like I had missed some crucial point, a long time ago.

I'd always had good hands, and I could weld, fit pipes, break down an engine, box, shoot, but I started to understand that certain skills had only ever constrained me, made me into a function, a utility. I hadn't really understood that until now.

My injuries kept me from working the farm that gives Angola its nickname. Jeanine helped get me the job in the library, as her assistant. She had mousy brown hair teased in a style that was out of fashion by the seventies, flabby arms that trembled when she stamped a card, and she lumbered when she moved. At times I would detect tears in her eyes and she would excuse herself to the back office and not come out until the end of the day.

I stacked shelves and pushed the cart down the cell block. Nobody much bothered me. Charlie Broedus was released in

'92, and I watched them come and go and pretty soon I was just a fixture there, in the stacks, at the lunch table, eyes on the page. All this reading increased my thinking. I could picture things in ways I hadn't been able to before. Like I've said, though—none of this made me a different person.

I know who I am.

I thought about Rocky too much. And I thought about Carmen. I wondered where she was, if she'd made it out. I never heard from her again.

Each day I imagined murdering Stan Ptitko, and I would think about the different ways to do it, getting up close and feeling the rattle, watching his eyes. Taking him out in the woods somewhere and making it last.

Each night I went to bed waiting for the cancer to thrive, but it just sat there, dormant, biding its time. I did nearly twelve years like that.

Just like that.

aroled right before the New Year of the new century, and I was alone in New Orleans when the clocks struck. Fifty-two years old, hitting the streets. Color schemes had changed in general, everything gone darker. Everyone had phones. People drove more Jap cars. Electronics were more widespread, TV screens everywhere. The Quarter looked just the same, the iron balconies and row houses and patios, the bars along the streets bursting with crowds. The piss smells and vomit in the gutters, the wail and bleat of the horns and thumping of the bass drums. People had been saying that everything might just shut down and stop working on New Year's, something about the computers. But I knew it wouldn't happen. I'd learned that after eleven years forced sobriety, I couldn't drink anymore. Alcohol made my liver twitch like an insect pinned to a wall. One more thing.

I stood in Spanish alcoves and watched the crowds churning through the streets, down Dauphine and Bourbon and Royal. Everybody kissed at midnight. Strangers sharing champagne bottles, lips pressed, hands stroking necks. Whenever someone glimpsed me watching from the shadows, they turned away.

I stayed in New Orleans because I was going to kill Stan Ptitko. His bar was still there, and its name was the same.

I spent a portion of my prison money buying a rod from a black kid on St. Bernard, and I started haunting the streets that fenced Stan's Place. It needed a pressure-washing, and a large piece of the tin roof was patched with blue tarp. A shallow ravine lay under a bridge to the northeast a few blocks, and I camped there for three days and two nights. I slept under the bridge, watching the place, wrapped in an old sleeping bag and a beat-up flak jacket, a hooded shirt, old slacks and tennis shoes, all from Goodwill. I thought of Rocky and that trestle she had to walk under on the way home from school, and about that night she'd spent there alone.

On the second day I saw Stan climb out a black Lincoln. He was much thicker, especially around the middle, and his hair had thinned.

I looked around and checked the double-action .38 and walked the next block clutching it in my jacket pocket. Before I knew it I was standing across the street from the bar. I crouched beside an old phone pole off the sidewalk, the hood pulled down, and watched the sleek black car, the metal door at the entrance. Three other cars sat in the lot, and I didn't know how many people would be inside. I'd seen a few others go in before Stan, nobody I recognized.

A silver day with a rainy, arctic light, my breaths little tufts of white in the winter air. Even in the cold I was sweating.

Next door the lot was still vacant, its ditch choked with slime and wild red roses, empty forty-ounce bottles, brittle yellow newspaper. A short wall of brambles and shrubbery had grown over the low chain-link fence between the field and parking lot. A breeze blew over the lot and I nuzzled my face into the jacket. Being there was not easy. I kept thinking about leaving.

Eventually Stan stepped out again, alone. I could see his face clearly now, puffy and fallen, his forehead much higher, his chin doubled. He slouched in a white shirt and black pants, stood beside his car and cracked his back, stretched, looked away down toward town and the river. He glanced at me but didn't seem to think anything about it. Old bum by the telephone pole.

It would have been easy. All I had to do was cross the street.

I don't know if my body just remembered all the things they'd done to me, but terror clamped down on my balls, heart, and throat. I felt the cold metal of the gun in my hand and the idea of using it seemed suddenly impossible, the thought paralyzing. My body was sort of transfixed by this panic.

I had no idea I'd become so meek.

I just didn't want anybody to hurt me again.

So at some point I'd become a coward. Or I'd always been one, and only just realized it, and now, like everything else about me, my insides were on the surface, plain as day.

Stan climbed in the car and started the engine, the exhaust thick as clouds in the cold, swallowing the car. I stepped out from the rough wood of the pole, hugged my jacket around me as the Lincoln pulled out the lot. I stepped into the road, a little stunned that I was letting him go. I doubt he looked in the rearview mirror, but maybe he did. Maybe he noticed the shrinking figure that stood in the street, holding a gun.

I trudged across the vacant lot to the sidewalk on the other side of the bar. I tossed the pistol into a Dumpster, and I dragged my leg ten blocks to the bus station.

I wasn't supposed to leave the state, but I rode the buses all the way to Galveston.

've boarded up the windows on the bottom floor, and most of the places around us have done the same. Then the owners headed north in packed cars, some of them towing trailers or jury-rigged flatbeds. The president and governor have declared a state of emergency, and a mandatory evacuation's been issued. Ike, they say, is inevitable. Elements rouse and converge, funneling ash-colored clouds. The drizzling rain fires sideways, so I skip my morning walk. I don't check into the doughnut shop either. I started to pack a bag, but stopped. I sit on my couch and sip some hot tea and think about the man in the Jaguar, and I wonder why I lived through the night.

I start to tug on my overalls, but my leg is stiffer than usual from the storm and sitting up all night. I leave them lying on the floor, and Sage runs over and curls up on the smelly denim. The hotel doesn't have any guests now, obviously, and I find Cecil in the office. He faces the computer behind the counter, tracking weather patterns, and he cocks one eyebrow at the storm depicted on the monitor. The spiral of clouds shown there is actually too big to imagine; the idea has to be contained by the picture on the screen, the way time has to be contained by a story.

"Maybe you shouldn't stick around," Cecil says. "I think I might be liable if something happens to you."

"Nah. You're fine."

"I still kind of think it might pass us. Maybe clip us with high winds. No storm surge," he says, but I know that like me Cecil is having trouble finding a good reason to leave.

"Anything need doing?" I ask.

He shakes his head and tosses a hand toward the empty parking lot. "Hurricane holiday." I stand with him a minute and we watch the animation on the computer, a thermal image of a swirling mass expanding and swallowing the coast.

He looks me over like I have a secret. He says, "What about the girl?"

"What girl?"

"The pretty girl. Spill it, old-timer."

"Who?"

"She didn't catch you? You're popular. First the suit, now this chick. Good-looking lady. Young, brown hair? Said she was looking for you. Yesterday evening, early." He opens a drawer behind the counter and takes out an index card. "I told her you'd be working today, but I didn't say you had a room."

I take the index card, and I don't recognize the name on it. It's in Cecil's handwriting, with a phone number below it. "She didn't give you a first name?"

"No. I didn't think to ask."

I reread the card. "What did she say?"

"That she was trying to find you. Asked me to ask you to call her. She was hot. You should call her, man. If you don't call her, I am."

"What are you going to say?"

"I'm going to invite her out for a bite to eat."

"How old did she look?"

"Early twenties? Look, if you end up calling her, put in a good word for me."

"Sure," I say, and I have to turn away a little, because a damp trembling stirs in my good eye. I even feel it in my dead one.

"I think," Cecil says, nodding to the screen, "I think I'm going to go ahead and go. You might want to think about it. You could ride with me."

"I'm fine." I push through the door. The sky is a bubbling mass of slate, charcoal, pewter, and the wind whips palm fronds and sends litter flapping down the empty streets. The air seethes with electromagnetism, presses around me, like being underwater, in a sunken city. I lock my door and draw the shades. Sage whines.

The hunting knife sits on the counter and I contemplate its razor edge against the creased, freckled skin of my wrists. I place the knife in a drawer, and I feel like a moron for ever taking it out.

I reach up in my narrow closet to a small shelf there, and I pull down the manila folder that contains an X-ray they took of me in prison. You can see the specks hanging in my lungs like stars, like shrapnel blasted backward through time, and I feel like I've finally caught up to the moment the bomb goes off. I can feel it in the weather, in the woman's name on the index card. And there won't be any assassins, no killers coming to see me off.

I light up a roach and pinch it between my lips. It's cool and blue here now with the curtains closed and Sage rests beside my feet, her head between her paws and tail tucked down, so I know she feels it, too.

The woman must have paid the man in the black Jaguar to find me. So she's got money, I guess, and I'm glad for that.

I stay inside with my dog and watch the skies and don't do much of anything else except glance now and then at that old X-ray and pace and roll another spliff.

This woman, I think, will want a story. Probably she wants someone to explain her life. She would want to know what happened in those two weeks when she was three years old, when she was taken from home and saw the ocean and played on the beach and watched cartoons. And one day her sister disappeared. What must that have seemed like to a child, I wonder.

One long story, peopled with orphans.

I scratch Sage and she whimpers once. My skin itches under my patch, and I lift it. Tears soak my dead eye, and I smear them off my cheek.

So I was wrong when I told Rocky you could choose what you feel. It's not true. It's not even true that you can choose when you'll feel. All that happens is that the past clots like a cataract or scab, a scab of memory over your eyes. And one day the light breaks through.

I think about Carmen, and wonder again whether she made it out all right. I hope she found something else.

When it comes, my heart doesn't even skip, like I was always expecting the knock on my door. It's stunted, light, the sound of a nervous person who doesn't want to disturb.

I turn the knob without checking the peephole. The door creaks open onto a woman with desperate eyes, full of beauty. Behind her, gray storm scuds are peeling out to sea.

She has thick, light brown hair, and she wears jeans and a tight tan jacket. Cecil was right, she's very pretty. More than pretty. She stands on the landing with one hand at her purse, a nice leather piece, and holds in her other a square of paper, a photograph, maybe, and instantly I can tell that there is a fundamental void about her. She aims for me to fill it.

"Mr. Cady?" She stares at me, a little cockeyed.

I step back and think to myself that she looks like a capable woman, someone with money, a life, a person who takes care of herself, and I'm glad to see it. Her lips are parted like she's waiting for words to come, while her eyes quiver between my face and the photo in her hand, searching. Such desperation.

"I don't recognize you," Tiffany says. Her voice is deeper, but almost recognizable, really. She looks back and forth from the picture to my face. "No. It's not you." She holds out the photo, offering it to me.

The picture is old, bent and faded. It shows the ocean, a beach. Three people stand out in the waves. The man is tall, broad and tan, and the girls are blond, lithe, their details lost in the white light off the Gulf.

I can actually see the child's face in this woman, the clipped chin and bold eyes, her bowed cupid lips. I ask her if she wants to come in.

"I don't . . ." She searches my face again. Thunder crackles and echoes over the sea. "I think I've made a mistake." She sighs. "I'm sorry. I came to the wrong place."

She takes back the photo and starts to slip it into her purse as she turns around, and I say, "It was twenty years ago. I've changed a lot."

She looks back, her brows arched, her stare brimming.

"You don't know me," I say. "But I was your friend."

A pin-sized tear skips down her cheek. I move aside from the door and motion her inside. Sage runs to her calves, and she crouches to scratch the dog's ears.

I invite her to sit. "Do you want some coffee, tea?"

"No, thank you." She pauses, picks her lip in hesitation. "I'd just like to—if you have time. I'd like, just to talk. If that's all right."

"You have questions."

"Yes. Please. I—" Scanning the room, she shakes her head, like she can hardly believe she's arrived at this place.

"I think I'll make some tea."

I move to the stove and turn on the burner, fill the teapot and set it atop blue flames. She left the photo on the counter, and I wash up at the sink as an excuse not to step back into the main room with her. In the picture I am brown and strong, like a horse in the sunlight. Icy water flows over my fingers, aching the joints. I can barely grasp the reality of this woman on my couch, the unlikely fortune of her existence.

She deserves better than the truth.

I step back into the room, met by Tiffany's quick, intense face. She scratches Sage and tries not to stare at the X-ray on the couch. She looks at my chest.

"How'd you find me?"

"Oh. It was—the lady from the hotel? A long time ago? She said your real name was Roy. The sisters told me that. The man I hired found your prison records, and pictures. It took him awhile to sniff you out. He's been looking awhile. We weren't sure you were the one, though. You don't look the same."

"No, I don't." I watch her scan the apartment, the single room, the stacks of paperbacks, and I glimpse a kind of pity from her. I don't like that. "Where do you live?" I ask.

"Austin."

"What do you do there?"

"I do graphic design. Advertising stuff."

"Did you have to go to school for that?"

"Oh yeah. I went to school there. UT."

"Huh," I say, and I almost smile. "Who—where'd you grow up? Your family?"

"My parents adopted me through the Sisters of St. Joseph. I grew up in Tyler."

She looks me over some more, kind of cocks her head. She has a ring on one hand, but I can't tell what kind it is.

"You're married?"

She shakes her head. "Not yet. Maybe soon. I've been seeing somebody awhile, a long time."

"You're in love?"

"Um. Yes." She tugs a strand of hair and glances away, and I see Rocky in the gesture, see her so clearly that I have to turn my head. When I peek back, I realize how much she looks like her, and my throat constricts. They have nearly the same face, and it's almost too much to bear.

"That's good," I say, unable to meet her eyes. "That you're in love."

"He's the one who got me to—this. He urged me. To find out the truth."

"What does he do?"

"He—I'm sorry," she says, and I've made her nervous. She doesn't know what to make of this room, its cramped space, those X-rays sitting beside her. Her fingertips draw to her lips and she peers around as if there might be someone else in here. "Would you mind . . . I really feel—there are things I need to know." She fixes Rocky's eyes on me, full of suffering, shining like a saint's.

I move closer to the couch, hold up a hand. "I know. You're right. How much do you know?"

"I kind of remember my sister. A little. I remember us going to the beach. But—" She chokes back a bit of her composure. "But one day she just left me." Her lips tremble at the statement.

"No, no," I say. "It wasn't like that."

"What happened?"

"We were coming back for you right away. We were just going out for the night."

"But, then you were in New Orleans? You were in prison."

"Yes. That's right." I turn over my palms and look down at myself. "I got banged up. An accident. There was a warrant out on me."

"But—I don't *understand*. What happened when you left me?"

I keep my head down and watch Tiffany's hand stroke the dog.

She looks away and then back to me quickly. "Did you know her very well?" Her voice snags on these last two words—"My sister?"

"I think I did." I study the shades of Tiffany's long hair—a dry prairie in summer—her sharp cheeks and wide eyes. "What kind of advertising do you do?"

"Sorry? I-I design Web pages, company logos. Things like that."

"I been to Austin a few times. Long time ago. Barton Springs still there?"

"Yes. Um—you said, about an accident?"

"Good music in Austin, too. Do you like music?"

She tilts her head at me, seeking my face. It's so hard to look at her that I'm grateful when I hear the kettle's shrill whistle and I can step back into the kitchenette.

My chest hurts. My hand shakes, gripping the pot, and little bulbs of sizzling water spill onto the burner.

"Listen." I hear her from the other side of the wall. "I need to know." She coughs, stifles some grief.

I pour two mugs of Lipton and leave them to steep.

"Did you have any other sisters or brothers?" I ask. "Where you grew up?" She's so young, so real, my voice keeps tripping. Her whole face gapes with hunger.

She nods. "I had a little brother. He's adopted, too."

"What's his name?"

She throws a hand to her forehead and twists up her mouth. "I'm sorry—*why* won't you answer me? Please. I don't understand."

No more stalling then, and I understand that I don't have the stomach to keep her story from her.

If I give her the truth, then maybe I am released of its obligations. I can pass the truth to its rightful owner, and the frozen stars in my chest might finally ignite.

So I realize I'm not going to lie to her. I'm going to tell her everything. Rocky, her father, Sienkiewicz's house, the men from New Orleans and what they did.

I become scared for her, then. And I think, *That void will be filled, baby, but you're going to have to be so tough to bear it.*

Years you can't remember. Years like mysterious bruises.

All this time, I was your friend.

"All right." I scratch my mouth and mumble, "It's bad, though."

"What?" More tears well under her fresh scowl, fierce and strong.

I slide the X-rays to the floor and sit down beside her.

"I'll tell you all about her, what happened. All right? But I got a condition." I pat Sage's head to indicate my line of thought. "If I talk to you, then you have to leave. There's a storm coming and you have to get out of town. Now. Right after I'm done."

"Are you leaving? I can come back."

"No. I'll talk to you now. I'll tell you everything. But if I talk, you leave. And you do me a favor."

"What?"

"You take this dog with you."

"Uh—well . . . I don't—"

"That's the deal. The only one I'm offering."

She watches Sage and tilts her head, scratches her. "All right. Okay."

"You swear?"

"Yes. All right." She nods, wipes her eyes once more.

She's grown tall, with strong, chiseled bones, the kind of woman you stop to look at, and her red nails dig into Sage's cinnamon coat as she sniffles and waits for me.

"That other girl in the picture isn't your sister. She's your mother. You shouldn't blame her. She had a hard life." I reach out, sudden and clumsy, put my mangled hand on hers. "But she did a brave thing once."

My hand looks monstrous touching hers, but she lets me keep it there. Her stare bores into my good eye.

"She didn't leave you," I say. "It wasn't like that. You weren't abandoned."

She covers her mouth and her features kind of sink and collapse like a sand castle at high tide. I draw closer and place my other hand on her shoulder, because I can't really help myself. She squeezes my fingers. I let things wash over her, give her a moment. She'll need her strength for the rest of it.

When she's a little more together and I've brought her some tea, I begin again.

I tell her everything.

After she's gone I stand at the door and watch her herd Sage into the car, a sensible gold Toyota. She pauses before getting in, and the rain gives her an aura. She looks back up to me. I have to close the door and step inside until I hear the car drive off.

I picture her walking Sage along the white rock and clear waters that run through Austin, and I don't think about Rocky.

I think about a breeze feathering the surface of a lake, my mother's voice singing "A Poor Man's Roses."

My head is light, and my hands don't ache.

The gale whips the rain into stinging darts, and the clouds turn the afternoon dark as a widow's dress. The heavy air teems with ozone and seawater. It snaps and crackles into the distance, and flares pop over the ocean as if the sky had swallowed dynamite. At its heaving rim I can almost make out another darkness, a form of denser black slouching up from the horizon in a shape I can't imagine.

Branches scraping the boarded windows sound like something trying to claw its way inside, and the wind howls like the voice of that animal, a low, wounded moan.

It's been twenty years.

I was worried I'd live forever.

Acknowledgments

My deepest thanks to Henry Dunow and Colin Harrison for their faith, insights, and efforts on behalf of this book. I am also grateful to David Poindexter—scholar, gentleman, and friend to writers everywhere.

About the Author

Nic Pizzolatto was born in New Orleans and raised on Louisiana's Gulf Coast. His fiction has appeared in *The Atlantic, The Oxford American, Ploughshares, The Missouri Review, Best American Mystery Stories*, and several other publications. He is the author of a story collection, *Between Here and the Yellow Sea*, and his work has been a finalist for the National Magazine Award. He lives in Indiana with his wife and daughter. This is his first novel.